It's 1939—war is imminent for the people of Britain. It is becoming increasingly clear that every able bodied man will be needed on the battlefront, and that British women will have to take over the jobs the men left for military service. This is the narrative of Scottish women in particular—through their stories, their experiences, their sacrifices—how they not only kept Scotland and Britain alive, but helped change the course of history.

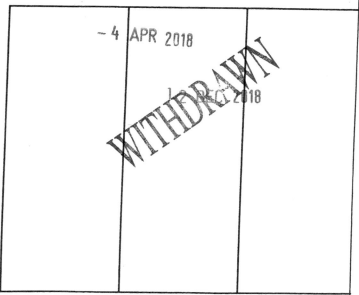

PAGE PUBLISHING, INC.
New York, NY

First originally published by Page Publishing, Inc. 2015

ISBN 978-1-68139-240-0 (pbk)
ISBN 978-1-68139-241-7 (digital)

Printed in the United States of America

CONTENTS

PREFACE

It's 1947, and we are finally on our way to America—Mom, my brother Tommy, sister Peggy, and me. Our whole family has descended upon Glasgow Central Train Station to say good-bye. Mom's three sisters are there: Nancy, Belle, Jean, and their husbands; all the cousins are there too—all are there to wish us a fond farewell. The excitement is overwhelming when Uncle Tommy Todd enters with his pipe band blaring away. As we pull out, I can still hear the music and exquisite voices of my family blending in perfect harmony, singing, "Now is the Hour"—giving us a true Scottish farewell. It is a day of mixed emotions, especially for Mom who is saying good-bye to her family; but also, going on a true adventure—a new life! My mother's sisters, Nancy and Belle, accompany us to London where they say their good-byes—"until we meet again." From London we train on to Southampton where we board the Queen Mary ocean liner for America. At the other end of our trip in New York City, we will be met by my father who had left Scotland eleven months prior to prepare for our emigration to America.

Fast forward sixty-one years to 2008. I am in New Jersey, USA, celebrating with over one hundred members of my high school class. It is our fiftieth HS reunion. I have not seen most of these people since I left high school, and it is quite an extraordinary experience. "What have you been doing these last fifty years?" Most of the answers, we, as women, gave to each other centered on family life. Generally, most were married with children and grandchildren and spent their lives as housewives. A few who, like me, continued their education and became nurses or teachers, but this was rare. While examining the 1958 Class Yearbook, I realized for the first time what the expectations were for most women in the 1950s. The country was still recovering from WWII and all the changes it brought. During the war years, women were in the workforce replacing the men who served in the military. At war's end, however, most returned to their role as housewives. "Women's Lib" was not in the vernacular of the times. In the United States, most women were still tied to the notion that a "women's place was in the home."

Typing was a required course for girls in my high school, but secretarial work was never in my future—my goal was to go to college. It never occurred to me to do anything else as I had big dreams and high expectations for myself. I discovered during that reunion conversation, there was obviously a disconnect between me and the rest of my classmates. I wasn't even aware that the 1950's societal mores had such poor expectations for young women. Born and raised in war ravaged Scotland, I grew up with a strong role model in my mother and the other women in my family. In the early years of WWII, Great Britain was standing alone—fighting off Hitler's attempt to consume, not only the British Isles, but Europe itself. The British government called upon every able bodied man to arms, leaving most of the women, elderly men and young boys to care for the soul of the country. This was a historical moment, the naissance of women's liberation. Most of the everyday jobs on the home front were taken over by grandmothers, mothers, sisters, aunts.

My aunt Nancy drove a Glasgow tram while my mother, the conductress, collected the fare; my aunt Belle served as an Air Raid Warden; my aunt Jean worked as a rail porter at the Glasgow Central Station. These were all "men's" jobs now being done by women. This was the message I received growing up: women can do anything!—and they did!

Through the years, I have worked as a teacher, business administrator, and a psychotherapist, never losing sight of my goals and the direction of my life. I was convinced there was nothing I couldn't do if I put my mind to it. I learned this lesson from my mother and my aunts, but it took some reflection of a life celebrating event to bring it to the fore. Looking back on that eventful day, pulling out of Glasgow's Central Train Station, I see what a brave woman my mother was. She had the courage to take that all important step and make a new life for her children. She, my aunts, and all the brave Scottish women who stood up, came forward and did whatever necessary to protect their country and their families are the *raison d'etre* for this book. I dedicate it to all of you.

DEDICATION

To my dear sister Peggy, my inspiration and support.
This book could not have been written without you.
You will be dearly missed, but I know you are going home.

Margaret Reid, Peggy Reid, Nancy Ferguson

"My heart is in the Highlands, my heart is not
here; my heart's in the Highlands wherever I go.
Wherever I wander, wherever I rove, the hills of
the Highlands forever I love."

—Rabbie Burns

INTRODUCTION

Writing this book has been both a challenge and a wonderful experience. Looking into the lives of some very young innocent girls who were called upon to do extraordinary things was incredible at the very least. What they did was unimaginable and astounding at times. Yet they did what they had to do without a second thought—without questioning themselves, but taking advantage of the situation and growing with the challenges. Why did I want to write this book, you might ask? I believe this book came to me and asked to be written. I was born in 1941 and grew up in the middle of a major life changing event. The world would never be the same after World War II. Not only did I live through it but was affected by the results of this event for the rest of my life. The history of WWII has always been an interest of mine. I have tasted it, worn it, felt it, and heard it through the voices of my parents, siblings, aunts, uncles, and cousins. Many stories have been told by them all through the years. It is a part of us all! What triggered my wanting to highlight the stories I heard was described in the preface—the "life celebrating event." Sometimes we need a jolt like that to put us on the path of enlightenment.

The initial process entailed comprehensive research. I wanted to know specifics about the war, the atmosphere in prewar Britain, life in Scotland, and in Glasgow—where I grew up. My research entailed reading books about WWII and magazines and newspapers from that era. Immediately it was apparent there was very little mentioned about the women's role during the war. I was astonished and angry! But also, the books I found that specifically wrote about the women's role, wrote only about English women. There were a few books written in the 1990s and early 2000 that talked about British women— Scottish, Welsh, and English. I felt very strongly that the Scottish women's voices deserved to be heard. This is what drove me! But I want to emphasize that this in no way diminishes the job that the

9

English and Welsh women performed and the sacrifices they gave. What I have tried to do is give recognition to the women of Scotland for their efforts and sacrifices, but through their voices.

The next step in this process was to find Scottish women who actually served during the war years. This was not an easy task as many of the women from that era had passed away. I began my search through my family, and friends of my family in Scotland and the United States. The word got out quickly. My cousin, Joyce, from Glasgow, contacted me with great news. Her best friend's mom served in the Women's Timber Corps—would I like to speak to her? Joyce gave me my first interviewee—Chrissie Morrison. Then while doing research in Glasgow at the Mitchell Library, I met a young woman who worked at the library, Lyndsey Weir. Lyndsey's mom also served in the Women's Timber Corps and she knew her mom would love to speak to me about her years in the WTC. It was remarkable how one lead led to another. Mary Weir told me about Rosalind Elders who introduced me to three other women who also served in the Timber Corps. From 2009 to 2011, I was able to interview sixteen Scottish women in their homes in Scotland.

Meanwhile, I wanted to take advantage of the fact that there were many Scots who immigrated to the United States and Canada after the war. Since I was also living in the United States, I thought I could find a way to seek them out. My sister Margaret was very much a part of putting this book together. She accompanied me to Scotland to help with the research and also interviewed some of the women when I couldn't make the trip. Margaret, who goes by the name of Peggy and lives in California, was able to find a number of Scottish women with the help of her good friend, Mary Scharosch. Mary's mother and aunt served during the war and although they had both passed away, Mary was able to pass along some marvelous stories she had learned from them. Mary also introduced us to some of her mother's friends who were willing to share their war experiences.

The final piece of this process was: I discovered a way to find some of the Scottish women immigrants in the US through the Daughters of Scotia, an organization in the United States run by Scottish women. The Daughters of Scotia (DOS) are organized into groups called Lodges found throughout the United States. The head of a Lodge is called the Chief Daughter and the head of all the Lodges is called the Grand Chief Daughter. My mother and her two sisters, Belle and Nancy, were all members of the Daughters of Scotia and all became Chief Daughters of different Lodges. My sister, Peggy, and my two cousins, Jean and Sadie, were also members. Peggy went on to become a Chief Daughter. Using these family connections to the Daughters of Scotia, I put together an inquiry and placed it in the DOS newsletter. This newsletter went out to dozens of Lodges throughout the United States. I received answers from women in California, Florida, Pennsylvania, and Michigan—most were not old enough to have served in WWII but whose mothers or aunts had. I either interviewed them face-to-face, on the telephone, or they emailed me with information. One of the women emailed me about her eighty-five-year-old aunt who lives in Aberdeen, Scotland—Lucy Findlay Burns. We set up an interview the next time I was in Scotland. Lucy was very special—alert, bright, and feisty. I interviewed her in her home in Aberdeen. An incredible experience! Everyone I interviewed, on the telephone or in person, was recorded with the exception of one woman who felt uncomfortable being recorded. My sister later transcribed all the interviews making it easier to access each person's words.

Finding all these women willing and able to tell their stories of their service in the war was remarkable! The youngest was eighty-four years old and the eldest ninety-seven. Some were extremely sharp, never missing a beat. But, also, making connection with the daughters of the women who served and hearing their experiences was not only exhilarating, but absolutely awe inspiring. All came alive while describing that special time in their lives. At this time in their lives, they all know they accomplished so much more than they had ever dreamed possible—yet, at the time of the war, "they just got on wae it!"

I hope you all not only enjoy the women's stories, but appreciate and recognize what they actually accomplished. For if it weren't for *all* the British women and their sacrifices and hard work, the world would be a very different place today!

CHAPTER 1
SHE DISNAE WORK!

Pre-World War II life in Britain was hard. The return of our soldiers from France in 1919 created a morass of cheap labor. In too many cases, these young men suffered from fragile physical and mental health. As a result, there were too many unemployed men and not enough jobs. The subsequent baby boom compounded the crisis. Jobs were scarce, productivity low, and rationing of food and fuel was commonplace. Britain was in the throes of the Great Depression.

With the continual growth of the British population (England, Scotland, and Wales) emphasis was placed on creating jobs for men. Although half the population consisted of women, a woman's place was in the home and therefore putting women to work was not a priority. Prior to and during the Great War, Scotland's major cities were industrial giants. Countless people were employed building ships, trucks, and military equipment for the war effort. After the war these jobs disappeared, they were no longer needed! Then, between 1932 and 1936, 2,688 factories were constructed in Britain—but only 102 of which were built in Scotland, which had a population of approximately five million. Consequently, Scotland's unemployment rate reached 16 percent. Major changes needed to be made in all of Britain. Unfortunately, it took another World War to make that happen.

By the late 1930's, Nazi Germany, driven by their dictator Adolf Hitler, was determined to rule the world. The Germans were slowly taking over small countries in Europe with an eye on Poland. The British government, watching and preparing, made it clear to the British people that war was imminent and that every able bodied man would be asked to serve his country. There was even talk in the House of Commons that women might also be called upon to serve as they did in the Great War. The jobs proposed were limited as most of the men and even some women in the House were of the mind that British women were incapable of handling jobs they considered too physical or that required more complex thinking. Work proposed for women were primarily cooking, typing, sewing, and knitting with the possibility of some industrial jobs in textiles or light metal trades. Yet, at this time, there were British women who were already working as doctors and nurses; as accountants, advertisers, architects, and solicitors. And some even served in the House of Commons. This must have seemed like an aberration to the people in power as very little recognition was given to the possibility that women could not only help the country but play a major role in the outcome of the war.

The fact that British women were encouraged to volunteer during the Great War and that many enjoyed great success did stimulate more interest and support for women in the post war society. Unfortunately, the Great Depression reversed many of these advances. It was extremely difficult to break the mind-set of not only the men of the era but many of the women—who would commonly say about their sisters, mothers, and aunts and wives—"*she disnae work.*" Meanwhile "She" is working endless hours running the household, doing housework, knitting, cooking, sewing, caring for her children, and often an elderly parent. Compounding this constricted thinking were the oppressive and confrontational trade unions, which legally—as they were supported by the British Parliament—kept women from working or taking a man's job. The unions were extremely powerful, insisting, on not only limiting a women's participation in the workforce, but also limiting their pay. Women received half the pay a man was given for the same job.

This extreme prejudice toward women in the workforce would require a major threat to Britain and its people in order for a more equalitarian sense to prevail. With the impending war, there would come a major shift in the world—a major change in the way people thought and an extraordinarily new way of viewing women—*including how women viewed themselves.*

By late 1938, the actuality of war was becoming abundantly obvious to those in power in the British government. Under the

13

threat of possibly being unprepared, there was much debate as to the roles that women would play. Finally, Parliament voted for the inclusion of women in the workforce. Single British women, ages 17 ½ to 25, were asked to volunteer for jobs that soon would be vacated by the men called up for military service. As most women were unemployed, there was an immediate response. Most of the volunteers sought jobs in the Women's Land Army and Timber Corps—especially in Scotland as the Scottish Land Army had recently been reformed and updated from the Great War. Other preferred jobs were in Civil Defense, parts of Air Raid Precautions (ARP), and the Fire Service.

Of all the women I interviewed, Rosalind Elder was the youngest to volunteer for service. She wanted desperately to be involved in the war effort, but also to be part of "something special." As it turns out, Rosalind made something special of the Women's Timber Corps. She became one of its strongest advocates through the years—fighting for recognition of the WTC's work and service to their country—a champion for the WTC!

> *I tried to get into the Air Force because I had a sister in the WAAF—I called and tried to enlist but they asked me for my birth certificate and of course I couldn't produce it because you had to be seventeen and a half and I was only sixteen. I went and shopped around to all the different services to see which one would take me. The only one that would take me without asking for a birth certificate was the Timber Corps. I thought I was all set, but, oh what a shock, it was when I got there. To see how things were going to be, living in a little wooden hut in the North of Scotland out in the woods. Most of us were Glasgow girls! And Edinburgh. But we got along fine with each other, yes we did. (Elder: BC Canada, March 2011)*

The Scottish people took the possibility of war very seriously. With the history of the Great War behind them, and given the relevancy of Scotland's tradition as ship builders and its munitions factories on Clydebank, they knew they had an important part to play. The River Clyde was in a strategic area just north of Glasgow, a major industrial city with a large population; but more importantly, the port at Clydebank gave British ships excellent access to the North Atlantic and the North Sea thus providing added protection for the country. The significance of the Glasgow/Clydebank area to any war effort also meant increased vulnerability to bombing attacks. This knowledge put the Scots on perpetual high alert, preparing well for the protection of their women, children and elderly folk.

October 1938 began a recruiting campaign for ARP. Men and women were asked to volunteer as Air Raid Wardens (ARWs), women as ambulance drivers and aides in first aid posts. Initially, men and women over age thirty-five were asked to be ARWs; those over age thirty, to fill first aid posts. The ARP Committee of Glasgow soon decided there was a need for a women's ARP department. The need was such that recruitment was taken directly to the working class tenement areas of Glasgow. "Kitchen Meetings," as these recruiting sessions were called, proved quite effective in acquiring the interest of housewives who would otherwise not have been considered or contacted by the ARP department. By April of 1939 over five thousand women volunteered in Glasgow for first aid training. By June of that year, 1,099 women had volunteered as ARWs; 3,003 women volunteered for first aid posts; and eighty-seven women volunteered as ambulance drivers. This was just the beginning.

The Great War introduced British women to the uniformed services, giving them the opportunity to voluntarily serve without actually being in combat. These services were the Women's Auxiliary Army Corps (WAAC), Women's Royal Naval Service (WRNS), and the Women's Auxiliary Air Force (WAAF). The jobs done by these women were indicative of the times. They worked as clerks, waitresses, chauffeurs, cooks, instructors, store keepers, and *telephonists*—all the services that were disbanded after the Great War as being unnecessary.

In anticipation that Britain would require the services of women when the country went to war, these uniformed services were reformed under the name of Auxiliary Services.

- WAAC reformed in 1938 as Auxiliary Territorial Service (ATS)
  The early volunteers who joined ATS were used as drivers, in clerical work and general duty, but once war was declared,

they were called upon for more serious jobs, i.e., part of the British Expeditiary Force in France.

- Women's Royal Navy Services (WRNS) reformed April 1939
  Generally, women age eighteen to fifty near naval ports applied for this service. They were asked to perform general duties such as drivers, clerks, cooks, etc. Eventually, these heroines performed such critical jobs as maintaining the ships of the Royal Navy. Many were involved in some of the most secret planning for D-Day.

- Women's Auxiliary Air Force (WAAF) reformed July 1939
  The WAAFs began as clerks and voluntary first aid nurses but it didn't take long before they were working in the Royal Observer Corps maintaining and flying barrage balloons. During the intense part of the war, they worked in Special Operations as saboteurs, couriers, and radio operators, and also as nurses in military field hospitals—at times near the front lines of battle.

Although the British government was pursuing all possible diplomatic solutions to prevent war with Nazi Germany, they continued to prepare for the worst possible scenarios. The final blow to Britain's efforts to avoid war came when Germany invaded Poland, in September 3, 1939. Great Britain and France—allies of Poland—declared war on Nazi Germany. Thousands of British men joined up leaving behind their wives, girlfriends, children, parents—and their jobs! Although, at this point, the urgent need for women volunteers was not yet on the horizon—young, single women continued to pursue a job. Their need for work, money, food, and be part of the war effort was urgent!

CHAPTER 2

PREPARING FOR WAR: KEEPING OUR CHILDREN SAFE

The threat of war was terrifying to the British people. Expectations of major bombings by the Luftwaffe was frightening especially in the major cities of London and Glasgow. Operation Pied Piper was formed in September 1939: a mass evacuations plan to move over three million people—mostly school children—away from the threat of enemy bombers. Families were to be separated—some for years— but the fear of losing their children in a bombing raid overcame their fear of separation. It was a very sad time for all.

In Scotland, the most vulnerable areas to bombing were Glasgow, Clydebank, Edinburgh, Rosyth, Dundee, Inverkeithing, and Queensferry. In Glasgow alone, over 175,000 children were taken from the security of their home to the countryside in Perthshire, Kintyre, and Rothesay. Although teachers from local schools acted as guardians for the evacuees being separated from their families was traumatic and painful for these young children. Glaswegians had a rough reputation in the outlying areas of Scotland. Mostly from poor, working class families the children of Glasgow were seen to be tough and combative. Going from city life to the countryside proved difficult at the very least for a Glaswegian child. Some were taken in and treated very lovingly but many were provided with little compassion. They were bullied, disrespected, and at times abused and forced to work. It was a contrast of cultures. The city life versus the country life—so very different and foreign to both—neither knowing how to deal with the other. It was a heartbreaking situation due to circumstances beyond their control and causing great pain to many of the children and their parents. The experiences of some of these children are voiced by the interviewees.

My brother was at Dunkirk, with our uncle and aunt, who lived in London caring for his children. During evacuation, the children were sent up to a farm in Glen Livit, but it was right out in the sticks. Aunt Peggy came up one time from London to see the children and she was horrified. They were just being used as slaves. They were working the fields, the whole day. There was no education or anything—it was cheap labor. My aunt Peggy said, "I'd rather the kids faced death down in London, than this." So she packed them up and took them home with her. (Burns: Aberdeen, Scotland, March 10, 2010)

I was only four and my mother was evacuated with me to Cupar, Fife, from our home in Edinburgh. We had IDs on our lapels, our gas masks, and off we went. Cupar, Fife, was a place where most folks retired and they didn't want city children. Of course, some of the tough kids from Glasgow and Edinburgh had to be hard to take, but they were not treated very well. I was lucky, I had my mother with me. She could only take living with strangers for a month and then we went home to Edinburgh. I think it was an enormous thing for parents to watch their children go off with strangers. Sometimes, they didn't know where they were until the children let them know. I have never seen anything like that since. I am seventy-four now and I remember it all. (Veldre, Sacramento, CA, November 8, 2009)

The day after the war was declared, we were evacuated—September 1939. We were lucky, our mom went with us, but we were separated once we got there. Nan and I were together, Rita and Jean were with mom. Ernie was on his own. You got a carrier bag and a wee tin of corned beef and biscuits, tea biscuits. You had to give this to the lady and you went to school just the same. We were going to Lochmaben, Dumfriesshire, it's near Lockerbie. We had to line up and when we got off the train they took us to the center of the town. We lined up again and all the people who were taking us were standing there.

Our names were called out and we had to go with this family. That's how we were all separated. Cathy's sister Nan said: "It wisnae hard for us, it was a wee village. We were always a close family. I was wi' Cathy. I wisnae losing anybody. They were nae losing anyone!" (Clark: Glasgow, Scotland, October 13, 2009)

Not all families were traumatized. Some were able to endure if they had a family member with them. Since evacuation was voluntary, some parents opted to keep their children home—especially if they were preschool age. Fortunately, my brother and sister and my aunt Nancy's two children were able to stay at home with our families. But unfortunately, my seven-year-old cousin Ella and her older siblings were evacuated to the Isle of Bute. But by Christmas of 1939, the feared German blitzkrieg hadn't happened and three quarters of the evacuees were allowed to return home. Ella and her siblings were some of the lucky ones, returning home after only three months. Children who were sent to Australia and Canada would not see their families for years. It was an unbearable situation—one that made an imprint on these children for the rest of their lives.

There would be a second evacuation in May of 1941, but that is a later story. Between these evacuations, there was so much that transpired, so many changes, so many significant decisions that influenced the outcome of the war and the lives of those who served and lived on the home front. The first evacuation planned was a symptom of the mindset of those in power. In attempting to prepare the people of Britain for the worst possible scenario, Parliament set in motion an ill-planned evacuation of all the children they thought would be in harm's way.

CHAPTER 3
TIMES THEY ARE A-CHANGING

Before war was declared, the British government depended upon British men to volunteer to fight for their country, but by September 1939, only 875,000 men had signed up. In April of '39, the British government tried to motivate young men into action by introducing the Military Training Act, which required six months of military training for all men between ages twenty and twenty-one. At the same time, the government enacted a very important document called *Reserved Occupations*—a document that would prove very telling in the conscription of women. This entailed the following:

Reserved Occupations: Dock Workers; Miners; Farmers; Scientists; Merchant Seaman; Railway Workers; and Utility Workers—Water, Gas, Electricity.

These occupations were *essential* to the war effort and therefore exempted the men working these jobs from being conscripted. Thus, in September of 1939, the British government announced that all men between ages eighteen and forty-one who were not working in Reserved Occupations could be called to join the armed services. Initially, all men ages twenty to twenty-three were conscripted and required to serve in the army, navy, or air force if they were *not* in Reserved Occupations.

Again, the importance of the women's role in the job market was downplayed most especially by the Labor Unions and even the new Prime Minister Winston Churchill. The British government continued to rely on women volunteers for nonessential jobs. In Scotland, there was a greater response to the call for volunteers. Unemployment was higher and the Scottish people were more attuned to the acuteness of the situation: Clydebank factories, ship building industry, food and timber demands—all in their own backyard. That Scotland had its own Women's Land Army gave credence to the fact that Scotland had the resources necessary—the farm land and great forests—to successfully support the war effort. This proved to be key to winning the war. Many of the women who volunteered went straight to the Land Army or Timber Corps whether they lived in the country or a big city.

I was about eighteen when I volunteered in the Timber Corps. It was very hard work—hard physical labor. Something entirely new and strange to most of the girls because we were mostly city girls. We actually felled trees and pulled them out. I drove the tractor. One of my friends drove a lorry. We worked side by side loading wood into the wagons. It was hard physical work. But I enjoyed it. (Armit: Kinross, Scotland, April 23, 2011)

I was seventeen when I volunteered for the Timber Corps and the thing came for my father to sign. My father said, "You are not going, and that's it!" So the first chance I had to go into Elgin where the Forestry Office was, I spoke to the boss. He says "You are very personable; we want someone like you, a country girl who knows what an axe is for." And I got the job to start on Thursday. Now I had to go home and break the news to my parents. I told my mother and she said you better tell your father. I went through and told him. He never spoke to me for three weeks, he was so angry. When I think of it now, you know, I had never done anything. I had no ambition and there were ten of us in the family and I was the oldest girl—I had one older brother. So here I am finally doing something! (Scotland: Edinburgh, Scotland, May 25, 2011)

I was seventeen when I volunteered. We were very poor, everybody was poor. It was the Depression, you see. Many men came back from the Great War knocking on doors selling books of matches—maybe a one legged man, oh it was sad to see. And he couldn't get work. An able bodied man couldn't get work. There was nae work. It really was a very, very bad time. Ye had tae stretch out everything tae get a meal. There was nae stretching left. Things were pretty dire! So I volunteered in the ATS. It was the great escape! (Burns)

Part of the reluctance to see the need for Conscripting women was the slow pace of war combat. In fact, September 1939 through May 1940 has been called the "Phony War" due to a lack of military action on both sides. However, once Winston Churchill became Prime Minister on May 10, 1940, Britain took on an increasingly proactive role. From this point forward, all of Britain—England, Scotland and Wales—was doggedly, determinedly immersed in "the War."

In the battle to save France, many lives were lost as well as ships, Royal Navy destroyers, and RAF aircraft. Fortunately, many lives were saved at the battle of Dunkirk because of the heroic efforts of ordinary people ferrying hundreds of soldiers in small, privately owned boats to waiting cruisers and destroyers—waiting to take them across the channel to England. Shortly after Dunkirk, France surrendered to Germany on June 22, 1940. Hitler assumed Britain would be next but Churchill and a majority of his cabinet refused to consider an armistice with Hitler. The evacuation of British and French soldiers at Dunkirk was a major emotional win for the Brits as it saved the core of the British Army. The Battle was on!

Hitler was determined to defeat the British one way or the other. They began Blitzing London and other critical cities during the dark hours—in an attempt to intimidate the populous. The Blitz continued through May of 1941; during this time, London was struck fifty-seven consecutive nights causing a loss of over thirty thousand people. There were, however, lesser known, but hugely significant bombings that occurred in Scotland as well. In March of '41, over 1,100 tons of high explosives and incendiary bombs were dropped on Clydebank and Glasgow—ports that were vital to Britain and the outcome of the war. The primary target was a highly industrial area where battleships, cruisers, destroyers, tanks, and munitions were manufactured. Unfortunately, large numbers of the workers were housed in nearby tenement buildings. By the time "the Scottish Blitz" was over about 1,200 civilians were dead, over 1,000 seriously injured and most of the tenement and public buildings destroyed. Over 50,000 people were left homeless. Even though the shipyards and munitions factories were back in full operation within a few weeks after the Blitz, the majority of the residents of Clydebank had to be resettled in another location and never did return.

The Blitzing of Clydebank and Glasgow devastated the people—frightening the populace—especially the children who continued to be traumatized night after night never knowing if the German planes flying overhead were meant for them. Air raids were held all through the war due to the continual harassment of German bombers raining fear over the Clydebank region. Often enough, they dropped bombs, but then most of the time they did not! But the norm was established and it was difficult to break the mind-set of the fearful children. That fear even inculcated the minds of the children living in Edinburgh.

> *Your queries and interest in the war has brought back so many memories of WWII in Edinburgh, Scotland. Glasgow and Clydebank were bombed to bits, especially Clydebank, but I remember the German bombers flying over Edinburgh. They had a sound that we all knew. We were bombed as well, but we thought it was the Luftwaffe getting rid of bombs on their way east and then south to Germany. I remember the nights in the shelters. The British spirit was alive and well in those shelters—women organizing games for children, and a lot of singing—helping us feel safe. As kids, we got used to women being in charge. It was the women who were keeping the country going!* (Veldre)

When I interviewed my cousin Ella in October 2009, she demonstrated the complicated and lasting effects of that fear:

> *One day I overheard my mother talking to a neighbor and she said that my father had told her "if the Germans land, be sure and turn the gas on and kill us all." So every time I heard the air raids, I thought if the Germans come, I'll listen to see if my mom turns on the gas. My mom always wondered why I never went to sleep during the air raids. But I was always listening for the gas.* (MacDonald: N. Ireland, October 16, 2009)

Ella cried throughout this telling of her story of the war. It was still a traumatic event to her, never knowing when the next bomb would drop.

My cousin Ella continued:

After Clydebank got bombed, we thought, "Well, they're going to come and get us now!" This was the big raid in the whole of Britain, that one! So they evacuated us again. I was nine then. When we went to the second evacuation it was quite a nice place. I liked it. It was in Lanarkshire; but, the people, mostly the kids, treated us worse than if we had been Germans. They used to chase us through the street and say, "That's those evacuees from Glasgow," and get sticks and run after us and throw stones at us. (MacDonald)

Fear of more bombings and increased possibility of harm to the children of Scotland brought on the second evacuation. However, because of the poor treatment that many of the children from Glasgow experienced the first time, the number of Glaswegian children evacuated decreased dramatically.

Nancy Black describes how the Clydebank Blitz affected even the people of Oban.

We got evacuees from Glasgow. The night of the Clydebank Blitz, they were just coming off the train with nothing. Nothing but their clothes, just to get away. It was pathetic to see them. My father went to the police station that night and found a mother and baby who had walked on the train and came off on this end (Oban), so he took them home. She was on her way to stay with relatives on Lochaline. Until she got the boat, she stayed with us. (Black: Oban, Scotland, March 3, 2010)

Some people were fortunate to be evacuated to a family member's home or a friend's home away from the bombing attacks. My brother and sister along with my mother, who was pregnant with me, left Glasgow right after the Clydebank Blitz—taking two different buses to get to Fauldhouse, a small town located between Glasgow and Edinburgh.

We were evacuated to our friends, the Mutters, in Fauldhouse. During our nine months there, life took on a pattern of normalcy and we went to school; ate hot bread rolls which were delivered by a horse drawn carriage; and Walter

Mutter wrung a chicken's head for dinner. My wee sister, who was born there, slept in a bottom drawer of a dresser in our bedroom. (Reid: Ayr, Scotland, June 26, 2012)

My cousins, Jean and Sarah Ferguson—my mother's sister Nancy's children, were evacuated to Fauldhouse too, but stayed with another family. My aunt Nancy stayed in Glasgow with her mother, our "Granny Brown."

Sadie and I, along with our cousins Tommy and Peggy Reid, were evacuated to a little town in a coal mining region called Fauldhouse. We were housed with a family with several children. We were taken care of and fed very well, and had a lot of freedom (since it was during school holiday). Aunt Margaret was also evacuated with us since she was pregnant with her third child. Jeanette was born, June 1941, in Fauldhouse. Sadie and I remember going for a walk into town with the other children, and coming upon gooseberry bushes. We decided to gather some, and of course, eat them while we did. We heard that gooseberries made good pies. Well I don't know about pies, but we both got deathly ill, and we haven't eaten a gooseberry to this day. (Caloz: New Jersey, July 25, 2009)

With the Battle of Britain, Dunkirk, the London and Clydebank Blitz's, Britain was fighting for its life! And the war was beginning to expand. Italy had joined Germany in its pursuit of world dominance. There were now many fronts to the war—Norway, Sweden, France, Italy, and Russia—putting a great deal of strain on the British military force—limiting the strength of the military. More men were needed for battle! Changes had to be made and it took a secret report by Sir William Beveridge in late 1940 to reverse the thinking of the people in government.

"It spelled out the looming labor crisis in hard figures. Men would be required in increasing numbers in civil defense and the armed forces. To meet this need, they would have to be withdrawn from industries, most crucially munitions, which would itself have to expand to meet the growing wartime demand. The shortfall was frankly enormous: one and a half million women would have to be added to the workforce to maintain production at the necessary levels." (Women at War, Margaret Goldsmith)

Despite this crisis, it would take another six months for the British Parliament to even consider the possibility of women taking over men's jobs. It wasn't until the Spring of 1941 under the Registration for Employment Order that every woman in Britain, aged eighteen to sixty, was required to register for work. The first step had been taken!

CHAPTER 4
DAE YE REALLY NEED ME?

It took another six months for the conscription of women to be legal. In December of 1941, the National Service Act (no2) was passed. Initially, single women aged between twenty and thirty were conscripted. But here was the major shift in thinking: Although women were not allowed to take part in combat, *they were required to take up work in Reserved Occupations—especially factories and farming to enable men to be drafted into the service.* Back in 1939, these jobs were considered essential to the war effort and strictly men's jobs. But in two years, it was becoming abundantly clear that every able body man was needed for combat duty in order for Britain to survive. Thus, those "reserved occupations" were reluctantly given over to women so that the men could be released for duty. In order for this critical transformation to be realized, the British government made a deal with the trade unions: when men returned home from serving in the war, their jobs would be available to them. The women would be required to relinquish their hard fought jobs and return to housework. Also, women would be paid half the salary men made for doing the same job.

It is apparent that "allowing" women to help in the war effort was a difficult decision for many—including the Prime Minister—and therefore the progression was made in small increments. The next step came in February 1942, when all women aged between eighteen and sixty, married or single, with or without children, *were required* to register with the Ministry of Labor. I would imagine the naysayers realized they actually needed the women's help if we were going to survive!

Some of the interviewees describe how the new ruling affected their lives.

I got married in January and I didn't have my honey-moon, but went down to Cornwall to be with my husband until July. When I came back, I had my lovely surprise and my papers were waiting for me. I had to go into munitions—that or the Land Army but I had too many allergies. I was nineteen when I had to go into munitions—we made Howitzer shells. We worked at Stewarts and Lloyds' where they made steel which we made into Howitzer shells. Plus I was also putting out incendiary bombs because I was an Air Raid Warden and that was part of my job too. (Clark: Dearborn, Michigan, December 8, 2009)

I was called up like everybody else. I was nineteen. When I went for my interview, I wanted the forces but they weren't taking women for the forces at that particular time as they closed every so often to get their papers up-to-date. They were going to send me to munitions, but I couldn't have gone to munitions as I can't stand noise. Then a girl in the office told me about the Women's Timber Corps. And I said, "Oh that will do me!" (Brash: Glasgow, Scotland, June 2, 2011)

Well, in 1940, I joined the NAAFI. That's the Navy, Army, Air Force Institute and I worked in the canteen in the aerodrome in Wick for a year, then to Castletown for another year. Then there was the conscription and the women had to join the service or go into munitions so I joined the service. In 1942, I was twenty-one years old and I went to Inverness to register. Two weeks after that, I was called up. I did my training in the Cameron Barracks in Inverness, then to South England for more training then to Whitby in Yorkshire. I was in the Ack Ack unit, and I served until they asked for volunteers to go overseas. I volunteered because they wanted the women to take over the men's jobs so they could go to the frontline. I was attached to the Military Police in France, and I was there for a while and as the war progressed, into Germany, then into Belgium where I stayed until the end of the war. It was an interesting experience but it really was a good life! It was a good life. There was six in our family, I went into the army, my two sisters went into munitions. Of my three brothers—two went into the Navy, and one went into the army. We all got home Scot free! (Cowie: E. Hanover, NJ, September 21, 2011)

Margaret Cowie, NAAFI

At seventeen, my aunt Anne Nimmo was given the choice by the government of either going into the service or working in a munitions plant in England. She joined the WAAF. She used to tell me about some of her adventures which I always thought were wonderful. One of her jobs included packing parachutes, and her final job was refueling airplanes at an English airfield just outside of Dover. The command would call her barracks and she would bicycle to the airstrip and fill up a fighter plane or bomber. The field was just a temporary airfield for pilots who were running out of fuel and could not make it back to their squadron headquarters. She spent many nights waiting for the planes and enjoyed chatting up the pilots while refueling. (Scharosch: Sacramento, Calif, August 1, 2010)

When I was about seventeen or eighteen, I was called up to work in munitions. I had to go to Glasgow to train for munitions. There were about eight of us who went together through to Glasgow from Edinburgh for six weeks of training. We went up there and stayed for the week, Monday through Friday and came home on the weekend. Four of us shared a bedroom and the other four in another bedroom. When the training was over, we were able to work in Edinburgh which was much better than travelling to Glasgow. (Tompkins: Sacramento, CA, December 24, 2009)

The response to the conscription of the British women was overwhelmingly positive, as indicated by the thirty Scottish women interviewed for this book. Most of those interviewed actually served in some capacity during the war. The remainder of those interviewed were the daughters of women who served, but were too young themselves to volunteer. Practically, every conceivable job was filled by women so that men could be released to serve in the military.

- Six women served in the Timber Corps
- One in the Land Army
- Three in NAAFI—one of whom served in the Military Police in France and Begium, and one who was also in the WTC
- Three in Munitions Factories
- One Porter at the Glasgow Train Station and factory worker (my aunt Jean)
- Two Air Raid Wardens—one was my aunt Belle
- One PBX Telephone Operator
- Five in the ATS—one at Bletchley Park as a decoder, one at Greenoch as a cipherer, two as lorry drivers, and one in munitions
- One took a man's job in the fish market as a Fish Monger
- One Tram driver (my aunt Nancy)
- One Tram conductress—"a clippie" (my mother)
- One served in the WRNS

- One lorry driver
- One ran boats out to convoys to transport some of the staff
- Two served in WAAF—one as a lorry driver, the other packed parachutes and refueled airplanes.

Twelve of the women interviewed were from Glasgow, five from Oban; the others from Aberdeen, Dollar, Paisley, Kinross, Point Jordan, Elgin, and Edinburgh. The diverse jobs performed by these women and the various location of their residency give a striking profile of the Scottish women who served their country. This profile indicates the strength, capability, and extent of dedication these women had. By mid-1943, 90% of single women ages eighteen to forty, and 80% of married women were employed in the forces or in industry in Great Britain. In Scotland, that accounted for approximately one and half million Scottish women fighting for their country. This far outnumbered the women employed in the Great War. This represents the tremendous response of the women of Scotland, England, and Wales to the plight their homeland was experiencing. What this book attempts to show firsthand are the words and insight of the Scottish women who served during WWII. The following chapters will delve into the actual experiences of these women, the impact on them, and how it changed their lives.

CHAPTER 5

WOMEN OF OBAN

Today, Oban is a lovely little beach town on the western coast of Scotland where many people go for a peaceful holiday. Back in the war years, Oban Bay and the "wee" town of Oban was the center of Royal Navy activity along with convoys from the United States and Russia. *Oban*, or *An t-Oban* in Gaelic, meaning the Little Bay, is called "the Gateway to the Isles"—to the inner and outer Hebrides. During the war, Oban Bay provided the Royal Navy and the Allies access to the North Atlantic and northern Europe—all very strategic. But it also gave the German Navy access to Britain and the Atlantic by way of Norway. German submarines were a major tactical vehicle for the German Navy especially in the North Atlantic.

By 1940, the significance of Oban Bay brought on a major decision by the British Admiralty—that Oban Bay be used as an additional naval base to the Kyle of Lochalsh. In order to ward off the possibilities of German submarines destroying merchant ships and convoys that sailed through the area, the Royal Navy built harbor defense control huts and two antisubmarine indicator loop defenses. Antisubmarine "indicator loops" are long lengths of cable laid on the seabed in shipping channels. When a ship or submarine sails over the cable a small current is produced in a loop. This current is detected by galvanometers at a Loop Control Station on the shore. This technology was developed by the British in 1915 and deployed at Scapa Flow in the Orkney Islands at the northern tip of Scotland, and since then has been used throughout the world as an antisubmarine defense.

To strengthen the defense of Oban Bay, besides the two indicator loops, seven control huts and a radar tower were built on the Ganavan headland, outside Oban overlooking Oban Bay. The defense huts included a Loop Control Hut, a plotting room, gun emplacements, and ammunition stores. This stronghold of the Royal Navy brought many changes to the small town of Oban. Before the war, the population numbered six thousand well into the war, with the influx of military personnel and the many Merchant ships, convoys, and destroyers, the population swelled to over twenty thousand, putting a great deal of responsibility to the townspeople, most especially the women. The women of Oban played a major role in the war effort giving of themselves in many ways. They have many tales to tell!

The Black Family: Donald and Barbara Black and their four daughters, Nancy, Isobel, Curstan and Catherine, very much a typical family in the town of Oban, were dedicated to the war effort, and did whatever was asked of them—and more. Mr. and Mrs. Black set the standard for their four daughters and took in evacuees from Glasgow and Clydebank, billeted soldiers and crew members of merchant ships. Mr. Black owned a butcher shop, and he was a administration officer for the distribution of food and an Air Raid Warden. Mrs. Black was a Billeting Officer for evacuee children and mothers with children from Glasgow. She also worked at the Red Cross sorting clothing to be given to shipwrecked sailors brought to Oban, and helped in the sailor's canteen in the evenings. Catherine, the eldest daughter, also helped at the sailor's canteen in the evenings and cooked for students doing forestry work during vacations from university. Curstan, the next eldest daughter, volunteered for the WAAFS in 1940 and was sent to Blackpool, England, for training. They wanted her to be a driver, but she had no experience as one so she was selected for training in meteorology and served until 1945. Both Catherine and Curstan had passed away by 2010 when I came to Oban to interview the Oban women. Only Isobel and Nancy remained to tell their family's story.

Isobel Black

In our family, we were brought up to help and work with charities—we used to go out on Flag Day, selling flags and things. My mother always encouraged us to do these sorts of things. She was in what they called the Townswomen's Guild where all the wives gathered together and learned different crafts, cooking and everything, how to make a meal for six-pence, that sort of thing. At the beginning of the war, we were all encouraged to join the Red Cross or volunteer at the canteens—we had three or four canteens in town.

Prior to WWII Isobel, nineteen at the time, volunteered in Air Raids Precautions, learned how to drive, and became an ARP driver until she was conscripted in 1943. She wanted to join the WRNS but "they had a full complement" so she was told she had to join the ATS. Because of her driving experience, she was officially a driver.

I was a driver. I drove anything and everything—ambulances, trucks, cars. We were given instruction in how to fix cars and trucks. I won't say we were all that efficient because we had all the workshops to deal with any big problems, but we did learn to change tires, have a look see if it had something to do with the petrol or something else. They did give us training—instruction in driving all kinds of vehicles: small Austin seven cars, fifteen cwt to ten ton trucks, ambulances, and Humber Snipe Staff cars.

Isobel began her training in Edinburgh, Scotland—but because of her previous driving experience, she was sent to the south of England to Camberley, the number one motor transport training unit. This is an important point! In interviewing these women, it became abundantly clear that the women were being placed in the jobs that best fit their talents and skills—a truly significant course of action to the outcome of the war. Most of the women conscripted were doing work they had never done before, *but* were utilizing skills that were well honed in their "everyday lives."

Secrecy was of the upmost importance in all aspects of one's job during the war. Isobel's work was extremely hush-hush.

After six weeks in Camberley, our commanding officer, Commander Wellesley, kept us in order and we weren't supposed to say where we were going; we didn't really know where we were going. We were told we might be going to Hereford, and you might be going somewhere else. So I had a secret indication for my family. I said I am hoping to see the Campbells and Mrs. Tebell who lived in Portsmouth, a friend of ours. So they knew I was going away down south anyway, but you weren't supposed to tell people you see. Careless Talks means lives so that was that!

After Camberley, I was sent to Edinburgh to join Number 6 antiaircraft group, that's the bow and arrow for the antiaircraft unit. They had "OUT" stations in the area all around where they had a medical officer to attend to the troops in the different antiaircraft sites. We drove the ambulance and their car. You were sent out for two months then back to headquarters and then you would go out to another one. We were there six months when the whole group was transferred to the South of England in preparation for D-Day. Six months before D-Day, they started preparations and our antiaircraft group was sent down to defend from Bournemouth to Eastbourne right along the coast. So we knew something was happening but never the details from our headquarters.

Isobel's work was becoming more secretive by the day–D-Day! Not knowing it at the time, Isobel and her female mates were in the middle of the most covert operation of the war—code named Operation Overlord—later known as the Battle of Normandy, which turned out to be the beginning of the end of Nazi Germany!

I was sent to Fort Fareham which was one of a ring of forts around Portsmouth built in the Napoleonic times in case there was an invasion from Napoleon, horrible places because they were built into the surrounding banks, grassy banks, they were underground really and General Eisenhower was in one of them, Fort Suttock, that was his headquarters with Montgomery, preparing for the invasion. That was quite near where we were. We used to see the Lysander Aircraft, very small, single engine aircraft that could land on a field and they would come in, either they were dropping spies from France or they were bringing back news from France to General Eisenhower at Fort Suttock.

The Allies—Britain, United States, and Canada, 156,000 strong—stormed the beaches of Normandy, France on June 6, 1944.

By the end of August 1944, the Allies had landed in Paris—driving the Germans out and freeing the people of France. Next stop was the invasion of Germany. Led by the Allied Commanders Omar Bradley, United States and Field Marshall Montgomery, Britain, the Allies crossed the Rhine River after smashing through the German fortified Siegfried Line and overran West Germany on May 7, 1945. Germany surrendered on May 8, 1945—officially known as VE-Day.

On the day of VE-Day, we were in this little unit and the medical officer was a lady and she said, "Now girls, just go up to the pub, take the tea out of your steel buckets and get them filled with beer! I'll pay for it and that'll do for the patients in this little hospital." So off we went in the ambulance to get these buckets of beer and we were coming back when a crowd of paratroopers arrived from their unit to have a celebration in this pub on VE-Day, and of course grabbed the girls and swirling them around and buckets of beer all over the place. So they had to pay to have our buckets filled again before we went back. That was quite funny that day. I don't think there is anything more exciting—we just had our duties to do every day going out with the medical officer to different units attending to those who were not seriously ill—those were the ones we dealt with as a rule.

Isobel Black experienced many things in her three and a half years as an ATS driver—life-changing experiences. During the interview, I asked her what her most stressful or traumatic experiences were.

Well, there was a lot of stress because you had to confront things that you wouldn't have been experiencing at home. Because we had no air raids here (in Oban) and the first air raid I was in was near Portsmouth and I had to stay the night on a gun site with my officer that I was taking and during the night, there was a raid and all the girls in the barrack room jumped up, hats on, trousers over their pajamas, and everything and OUT TO THE GUNS and I was left alone in this tin hut, didn't know where they had any shelters if they had any. They usually had ditches that you could run into. Didn't know where anything was so I just put a blanket over my head and hoped for the best. The shrapnel was coming down on the tin roof and oh, oh, oh, what will I do? And I just sat under the blanket and waited 'til the girls came back. They had to come back after being out for hours and they still had to report for duty at eight in the morning. Back on the guns! I admired them. They were wonderful girls, you know to do that all the time. We made some good friends. I kept in touch with quite a number of them, but they have all died off one by one. I am the last one left. I'll be ninety next month!

When I asked her: "What was the biggest thing that you got out of your experience?" Her reply was:

Relief that it was all over. It was just relief. You felt that you could go home, you wouldn't know what would happen next but at least you were free.

Isobel Black's attitude toward her job was always:

We just went out and did our duty. We just had to get on with it! (Isobel Black: Oban, Scotland, March 5, 2010)

Isobel Black, ATS, Official driver of Lorries,
ambulances, and staff cars

Nancy Black

Nancy, the youngest woman in the Black family, was twelve years old in 1939 and couldn't wait to be involved in the war effort. It wasn't until she was fifteen in 1942 that she was allowed to take on a job. With her father's direction, Nancy chose MacBraynes—the shipping agent in the region. MacBraynes became a major player in the organization of the continual flow of merchant ships and convoys in Oban Bay.

I chose MacBraynes because I was into boats a lot. I went as an office girl. The fellow who had been loading the stores for the convoys was called up, and there was nobody else so I ended up with the job. That was very interesting because it was the east coast fisherman who had what we called "drifters." These were requisitioned by the Admiralty and they were running stores and people out to the convoys. We were just kept busy with that all the time. The mail came in to our office and we took it to the customs for censoring and they sent it off after that. Skippers of the vessels came into our office. We had priority with phone calls 'cause ordinary people had to book well ahead to get a phone call through but we had priority. So we got the Skippers through to their owners where they got their orders on what to do, requested any stores they needed—then we ordered their groceries or vegetables or things like that. If they needed more then I saw that they were loaded onto the drifters.

Right from the beginning, Nancy's brightness shone through. She was given more and more responsibility, proving with each assignment how capable she was. Oban became a central location for the thousands of servicemen and women who poured into town daily. The Royal Naval Headquarters was located in one of the major hotels along the Esplanade in the center of town. Much was going on—most of which was confidential—making one's job difficult at times. But Nancy—in her fearless way—carried on.

You did anything you were asked to do! Went to the bank, collected three thousand pounds for a ship that was paying off, you know things like that. You just did anything. Actually, my boss was supposed to get me a pass so that I could get into the piers but never got around to it. All the sentries got to know me and I would just "walk through." I remember one day I was going into naval headquarters in the hotel along the front. There were naval officers coming out and they were just looking at me and I suppose the sentry would be quizzed when they got downstairs. "What was I doing in the naval headquarters?" But I had to go along to the administrator of the transport office to collect the secret file telling us which ships were going to be in at that time and I took it back to the office.

Oban was becoming increasingly busy with military personnel due to the influx of convoys gathering for trips to America, Russia, or West Africa. The convoys came by way of the Clyde and Liverpool as the Glasgow area was inundated with ships from the shipping industries. Thus Oban Bay and Loch Ewe became the two most important gathering places for the convoys.

We had so many people coming through. We had survivors come in, we had a clothing store and survivors were brought in, usually by the navy. They came in with nothing but a blanket, so we had to provide them with dry clothing and travel passes to go home. You see they didn't get any compensation from the Merchant Navy. Once their ship was torpedoed, they didn't get paid after that. Pretty hard going!

Food was another major issue for the people of Oban—not only for themselves and the military personnel stationed in Oban, but for the many survivors who were sent there for aid and support. Because of security measures, the townsfolk were limited—quarantined in a way—as to where they could go or where they could travel. Food was scarce and of minimal variety.

You didn't travel in those days. You didn't have the means except by bicycle, just as far as you could cycle. We used to go to gardens about seven or eight miles out because we knew somebody who knew the gardener and you could buy vegetables but that was really the only time we were out of town. You couldn't go to the islands at all because you needed a travel pass for that. My father had a butchers' business but this did not mean we had lots of extra meat. The ration provided to him allowed for loss in processing the meat and a good butcher could cut this down considerably, making more available for the customers. My father gave a little extra meat to all his customers. We never had roast beef or fillet steak at home as this was reserved for the hotels, but had, usually, a sheep's head, flank of mutton or tripe which many customers did not wish to accept as their ration. There were plenty of rabbits to supplement the meat ration so we were better off than other parts of the country.

Food was scarce throughout the British Isles; in fact, at one point in the war there was approximately two months' supply of food available in Great Britain. The saving grace came from the Women's Land Army, which, with hard work and dedication, more than doubled the output of food that had been available before the war. As indicated by Nancy, the location and circumstances at Oban Bay prevented the people of Oban from accessing the farmlands in the highlands and the food produced by the Land Army. Fortunately, Nancy was able to benefit—on some occasions—from the circumstances of her job.

One time, we got to know quite a few of the American skippers and one of them invited me for a visit on the convoy. The men of the drifters would say, "Oh come for a trip with us." But we were strictly forbidden. I asked permission from my boss and he said, "Oh yes you can go." So on my half day, I went off with them out to the convoy and we went around to the different ships dropping off the provisions. We then came to this American ship and they asked me on board. They gave me a meal in the officer's mess and I will always remember the sour kraut, which I had never seen before and the white bread! There were other lighter moments as well. We didn't have any fruit. I remember coming from the pier one day, and opening my desk and there was an orange. One of the skippers had put it in there for me.

Nancy tells another interesting story, one that wasn't verified until many years after the war, and by a very unusual source!

Do you see the beam behind the boat there down to the south (Nancy points out during the interview), *just over there they were farming. And this day my aunt was down in the hayfield below the farm at Gylen Park—near the water, when she heard a hissing sound—what sounded like air blowing out of a submarine's tanks as it came to the surface and then the sound of voices in a foreign language. She wondered, "Is it a submarine?" So she went and hid—stayed for a while wondering. She was on her own at the time with no telephone at the house and no transport. My aunt remembered that before the war there were a lot of German waiters who came to Oban to work in the hotels. Sometimes, they would hire a row boat and row around Kerrera. The story was that these men were taking soundings from all the bays and what was on the bottom. This information was all going back to Germany and they must have found that the bay was a good place for submarines to come in. That was the story my aunt told her husband—he didn't believe her—thinking it was just her imagination. But then the following day they heard depth charges going off down at Colonsay—which is south again and they thought it had something to do with what my aunt saw and heard, so my uncle came up to Oban to report it. Then years later, the owner of a bed and breakfast establishment near Oban was talking to one of his guests, a German, who had stayed with him previously. When the conversation turned to wartime, the guest mentioned that he had been aboard a submarine which had called in at the south end of Kerrera for water, knowing there was a small stream there coming from a spring and very few people residing in the vicinity. They came into Oban Bay on the east side of Gylen Castle. While busy filling the casks, they heard noises which made them think the home guard had discovered them and they dashed back to the submarine and moved quickly out of the bay. It turned out that the cause of the disturbance had been a herd of goats. The submarine proceeded to the north entrance to Oban Bay but were not sure of entering without detection and left without opening fire on any targets. My aunt's report was vindicated and Oban had been saved by our noisy, wee goats.*

There was a lot going on in Nancy's world but she weathered through it and learned so much especially about herself. When asked what she learned out of all that experience, she said:

Self-confidence! I think! The self-confidence that you could cope with anything. You learned a lot one way or another.

Then she went on to say:

It was something you had to live through. At the beginning of the war when there was a real threat of invasion, I was all ready to get hold of a rifle and take to the hills. Get as much food as I could. I don't know what the family was doing; but, that was what I was planning. It was just at that stage—I was twelve years old then. At one time, we only had three weeks' worth of food in the country. It was that bad! It was a near miss for us.

Nancy finished with this:

But it always amazes me, how we were able to get everything going to fight the war. You figure we were unprepared and yet we managed to pull everything together. I mean the civil servants that must have done all the organizing, the calling up and getting people together and finding the right people for the jobs. (Nancy Black: Oban, Scotland, March 5, 2010)

Margaret Harris

In 1940 Margaret Harris, age seventeen, volunteered for the WRNS. She was stationed outside of Oban in Greenwich, England to attend the Officers' Training Course.

The Officer's Training Course was only a fortnight. At the end of the fortnight, we were told where to go. I expected to be going somewhere else; but they said I had to stay for the cipher course. I thought I would be there for another fortnight but it turned out to be six months. Then we were told where we had to go. I was appointed to Greenock, Scotland. Of course when you arrive there, they're not expecting you or anything like that. Oh, we never heard you were coming and all this sort of thing. The minute you are in the cipher office in Greenock, they tell you to forget everything you were ever told in Greenwich, this is the way we will do it here. So I was there for four and half years doing ciphering. There were six people on watch—six all doing different things. I worked my way up—gradually becoming Head of the Watch. If there was anything happening in the invasion of North Africa or the invasion of France, you started getting messages from someone. If it was a "Hush message," only the Head of the Watch could work on it. When I was Head of the Watch, I had to leave everything that was my work and focus on the "Hush message." Then there was a series of steps that had to be taken: make six copies of the message and take them around personally to the Admiral, Chief of Staff, and anybody else of import. So your own work was left. Every other message was Hush but you really didn't know. You may be given routes of ships and you didn't have time to look them up on the map—you just had to do your best and write them out. It was very exciting too! Of course you got Hush messages about Churchill and Stalin – all meeting together somewhere, or Churchill meeting in the Atlantic. Of course you couldn't mention anything to family or friends at home. I knew an awful lot and I used to be worried in case I mentioned anything that was a secret.

Although exciting, the pressure of the job was "arduous" according to Margaret. All the women felt the pressure in many ways—it was hard to endure. Mistakes were made—exacerbating the situation.

We once sent a convoy to Gibraltar when it should have gone to Iran in North Africa. Nobody found out until the convoy arrived at Gibraltar and they had to send them along to Iran in North Africa. The war in North Africa was just finishing up so it probably was too late. I'll always remember the code number in ciphering for Gibraltar was 5004 and the code number for Iran was 5005. Someone had made a mistake. So they never, ever, ever, ever found out who for it was a Hush message in a Hush log and locked up! Three months later, the Admiral came in and said, "The message was placed from the cipher in Greenock, who did it?" They went through the log but they never did discover who did it. It was a mistake!

Whoever had done it, must have been out of the cipher log because everyone knew everyone else's writing. It was all hand written: whose shift it was on, whose watch it was on. But we never ever, ever found out! Nobody confessed! Nobody said, "It was me!"

Although both exciting and arduous, there were also many positive aspects to the job. Women made many friends, friends that have lasted over the years. Margaret was eighty-seven at the time of our interview and she still had contact with the women she made friends with during the war. Another affirmative aspect of their work was how well they were taken care of—in Margaret's words:

"We were very, very, well fed. We had lovely food. More or less waited on hand and foot!"

And the piece de resistance for Margaret was when she reached the "senior" level of ciphering.

There were some troop ships going across to America and I said I wanted to go. Because I was a senior, they let me go. I was posted on the Atlantic for six months—ciphering on board. Messages came in Morse code—they came in calligraphy and they were all figures and you undid them. I was on the Ile de France—a liner that became a troop ship. We had a wonderful time in the states, absolutely wonderful. Everybody made a terrible fuss of us. It was lovely! They took us for weekends to Greenwich, Conn. Families invited us out and we had a lovely time with them. For that six-month post on the Atlantic, I received the Atlantic Star medal. That was wonderful! Wonderful!

When asked what she discovered from her war time experience, Margaret replied:

I always regretted not going to university because I could have gone quite easily, why now I don't know. My daughters have all said to me the war was just as good as going to university for the experiences I got, the people I met in all walks of life. It was, I think, just like going to university! I also was able to go to London —something I had never done before. I went when I was quite young; that broadens your outlook! (Harris: Oban, Scotland, March 5, 2010)

Sheila Young

Sheila volunteered when she was seventeen years old in 1942 and wanted to do something exciting and travel at the same time. When she was conscripted at age eighteen, she joined the ATS.

> *Because I was working in a bank I was in a "reserve job" and I didn't need to go in the services, but when I turned seventeen, I thought I really wanted to go away in the forces. I think I had the travel bug even then. I thought it would be exciting and I wanted to go while I was a young girl. So I volunteered and as soon as I turned eighteen, got called up. In Oban, they had the WRNS and the WAAFS and I thought I don't want to join up and be stationed in Oban—I may as well stay in the bank! So I joined the ATS. I had also seen an exciting film at the time that was all about the ATS driving lorries and cars.*
>
> *My training was in North Wales where I attended driving school for three months. You learned on a different vehicle every day. One day you would be in staff cars, another day you would be driving ambulances and then lorries. A half day was spent driving and another half day in mechanics learning to maintain your vehicle. After three months there, I was sent to London and I was in London during the doodle bugs and the bombing—the V2 rockets. That's a bit scary—when you are driving, you don't hear them until they drop. Bumps in the road and one would drop near you. You never knew if you were going to be dead or alive. I think that was probably the scariest.*
>
> *When I was in London, I was driving the entertainment companies out to the country in a three-ton Lorry. After their show, I would drive them back at two or three in the morning in the blackout. I'd never been there before and got completely lost. The first night I did, it I was driving round and round. I had heard so many tales about things that happen that I wouldn't stop and ask anybody. Eventually, I had to stop and*

ask somebody. I opened up the window of the Lorry; held onto the door and put my head out and asked if someone could tell me where Kensington Barracks was. He replied, "No English, No English!" Fortunately, another vehicle then appeared. It was a Lorry with very light taillights. I thought, well I don't know where it's going, but I'll follow it. It was going into the barracks and I got back all right.

Sheila learned a lot in the early months of her stay in London—driving various types of vehicles to different locations with a variety of duties. As her experience broadened, she gained a reputation as a competent and trustworthy driver, which opened up a whole new world to her.

In just a couple of months, I got trusted to drive the Brigadier in an out station in Wimbledon. I became his personal driver—I was driving him and his staff in a lovely Humber—a beautiful car! My job was collecting officers at the station and taking them down for a course at the staff center. Once, I had to carry the Brigadier all the way to Eastbourne and to London. I did this particular job a while and then was promoted again. I went to an officer's training unit in Windsor and was driving the commandant there. All wonderful experiences, but my final year—my posting in Egypt—became a chance of a lifetime! I got to travel to a place I would never have had the opportunity to do if I hadn't been sent there. I drove a three-ton Lorry again and that was a case of going out early in the morning when it was fresher to pick up and deliver the food and supplies for the different units in town. My time was my own—out at five or six in the morning—finish by midday and then the rest of the day was my own. That was a bonus really, that was the good bit!

After a year in Egypt, Sheila came home in 1947 and was demobbed—returning to her "humdrum life" at the bank. Her words! She married in 1949 and settled down to married life and three children. Unfortunately, Sheila was widowed after twenty years but then returned to work as an office manager for AISO. She retired from there after twenty years, married again, and is living a wonderful life.

My final question to Sheila was: "What was the biggest thing you got out of your experience in the war?"

Well, I learned to be very independent. There was no one there, no shoulder to cry on if you weren't feeling good, if you were worried or frightened. And it was frightening! The first week I was in Kensington, there was a bomb in the back garden on the unit there. There were about seventy people killed. I was under the table in the basement with a tin hat on wondering why I left Oban—thinking this was not such a good idea. But it was a very good experience. I wouldn't have changed any of it. (Young: Oban, Scotland, March 5, 2010)

Sheila Young, ATS, Official driver for Brigadiers

Jay MacDonald

Jay was seventeen years old when she volunteered in 1943. She was going to university at the time—and realizing she was soon to be conscripted—she volunteered instead so she could have a choice as to where she was going. She had three possibilities and chose the ATS. Having had university experience brought her to the attention of the recruiters at ATS as they had come to realize that the more educated the volunteers, the more apt they would excel at a higher intelligence job. Jay was given further intelligence tests which revealed she had a special aptitude for being a wireless operator. Throughout the interview, Jay gave minimum information about how she was chosen for the job, and a modicum of detail regarding the work she proved invaluable at. This attitude was ingrained in the women who worked in top secret positions, especially in ciphering and decoding—that it was Hush-Hush. Jay makes that abundantly clear!

> *There were only three services, the WRNS, the WAAFS, and the ATS. Nobody here* (in Oban) *was in the WAAF and I suppose it was just vacancies at the time. You have to be at the right place at the right time. I got the ATS and went off to do basic training and then after basic training, I went as a Special Wireless Operator on the Isle of Man for six months. That's where we learned morse code and from there, I went to Harrowgate which was a big station, an intersect wireless station.* (Harrowgate was a secret wireless station where they intercepted enemy transmissions that were subsequently decrypted at Bletchley Park) *I was two and half years at Harrowgate and about another year at Beau Manor, another intersect wireless station 'til I was discharged December 1946. Very hush, hush the job that we had.*

Jay MacDonald spent three and half years in this secret world—intersecting German messages—not knowing what was in the messages, but having to correctly intercept the code. Although she never mentioned Bletchley Park, Jay MacDonald was later recognized as one of the outstanding cryptanalysts along with six hundred other women of Bletchley Park. They broke the secret Nazi codes, which eventually led to breaking the back of Nazi Germany!

Jay did admit, in her understated way, that her job did have some stress at times.

> *We worked in shifts and the shifts were quite hard going, you were on from one to seven one day, and the next day you were on from seven in the morning 'til lunchtime and then you were on again seven that evening 'til midnight. The shifts played havoc with your digestion and all sorts of things. They did take good care of us though. We all had good uniforms and*

the food was good, although there was always someone who complained about the food.

When asked the best thing about her experience, Jay replied:

It's a great University of Life. Great! Made such friend-ships, met so many people. I am still in touch with eight people. We are all so old now and my school friends have died off, but I can still find eight of the ATS. That tells you something, doesn't it? (MacDonald: Oban, Scotland, March 5, 2010)

Jay MacDonald, ATS, Cryptanalyst at Harrowgate

These are the women of Oban, five very different women who gave their all for their country and did whatever they had to in order for Britain to prevail. It was a remarkable experience for each of them. So much positive energy was spread throughout their lives because of what they learned: understanding, toughness, confidence, friendship and—most importantly—a new way of looking at themselves. They realized: "There wasn't anything they couldn't do!"

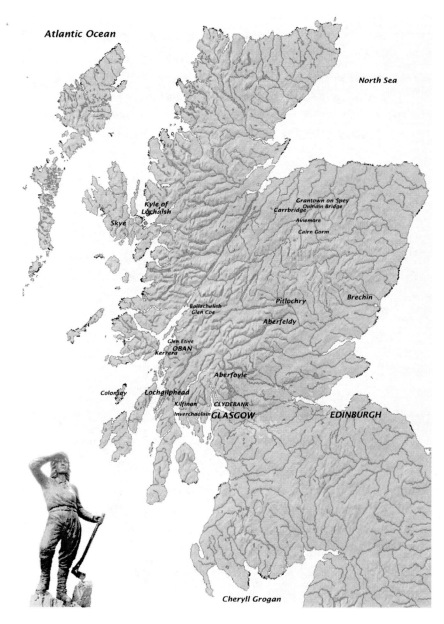

Map of Scottish Highlands highlighting where WTC
worked, and strategic areas surrounding Oban.

CHAPTER 6
WOMEN'S TIMBER CORPS

One of the hardest jobs, paid minimal wage, provided the greatest value to the war effort, and received the least amount of recognition. This is the story of the Women's Timber Corps, a sad one, but when all is said and done, the bravest and most heartwarming tale of all!

The Women's Timber Service was established during the Great War and was reinstated in April of 1942, as the Women's Timber Corps by the Ministry of Supply in England. Scotland formed its own Women's Timber Corps (WTC) as part of the Women's Land Army in May of 1942 with its own identity and uniform. Scotland's forests are world renowned for its quality and quantity—"breathtaking" is the word most commonly used to describe not only the views of the Scottish pine forests but also the beauty of the wood they produce. Not many people were—or are to this day—aware of the critical role Scotland's timber played in the war effort. In preparation for the war, the British government had acquired 1,444,000 acres of land in Britain and planted 434,000 acres of trees. Few of these forests would be mature enough to provide the necessary raw material for coal mines, munitions factories, shipyards, railway ties, telegraph poles, and eventually soldiers' coffins. One of the most essential products for wartime was the wood sent to charcoal kilns where it was burned and turned into charcoal. This charcoal was used mainly for explosives, gas mask filters, and smelting. It was imperative that already existing, mature forests be accessed. What was required and finally recognized as the most expeditious were the forests in the Grampian and Cairngorm Mountains of Scotland.

Scotland's formation of its own Women's Land Army and Timber Corps was a strong recognition of not only the imminent and crucial demand for timber but the dire urgency for women to take on the work of timber felling, working the sawmills, hauling wood—everything necessary to get the timber to where it was urgently needed. Also, and most importantly, this allowed men to be released for military service. Most of the women in the WTC came from cities and "never, ever"—as some of the women like to say—"picked up an axe in their lives." They had to learn to live under extreme circumstances, in a cold and frigid environment, with minimum opportunity for a warm bath, and a poor quality of food. Some of the women worked alongside Italian and German prisoners of war (POWs) who, at times, were better fed than they were. The interviews with the women of WTC tell of their experiences with the POWs and provide a telling glimpse of humanity. We also learned what it meant to these women to be able to serve their country and help the men at the frontline by supplying the wood necessary for their survival. The women of the Timber Corps were affectionately known as the Lumberjills. Here are their stories.

Grace Armit

I had been working as a waitress in Govan, Glasgow. I knew I was going to be called up but I couldn't take the discipline of the service. I wanted something different with a spirit of adventure so I volunteered for the Timber Corps when I was about eighteen or nineteen. I was sent to Shanford Lodge which had been an old shooting lodge and part of an estate at one time. There were huts but I was one of the lucky ones that got into the house. It was big, it was bare, it was cold, but you accepted it because there was a war on and that was it. There were good points as well as bad. You were absolutely isolated. You were away from town and the cities. It was austere; everything was very cold, everything was minimal, comfort was minimal, a bath was a luxury. This was an old shooting lodge so it wasn't up to date. It probably dated back to Queen Victoria's time. But it was good! There were about thirty of us in the house. We also had three huts where there must have been about twenty girls, I imagine. It was quite a big camp. It had been a training camp at one time but then they made it into a work camp. They needed the timber for the war. Yes, we made pit props and timber for ships. My job was felling trees. Sometimes there was a part of the wood that was overblown— trees were already half way down. The Italian prisoners pulled them out; they did the donkey work. I drove the tractor that pulled the trees out. My friend was a lorry driver. I worked alongside her; we loaded the lorry and took the work to the train station. We loaded the wood into the wagons; it was hard work physically. But I enjoyed it. It was good. It never did me any harm but we were paid a pittance.

Grace had some experiences with the POWs when they had to work together. Initially, it was with Italian POWs then as the war progressed, German POWs were sent to help the WTC.

We were really very much apart from the POWs. The Italians didn't like us. They didn't get much food, just as we didn't get much as the rations were very short. I remember one of the Italian POWs saying to me "You plenty food, me pris- oner, no food"—which wasn't true. But the Germans were very much afraid, I think. They were very, very careful and good workers, much better than the Italians. There was one who found out his wife and child had been killed in an air raid. He probably was heartbroken and angry. Seemingly, he was throwing logs at the girls and had to be taken away. In another incident I remember, when the war was coming to an end, the German POWs were all talking amongst themselves and I didn't know German that well, but I knew something was agitating them, and I said, "What's going on, what's wrong?" At their camp, they had been shown pictures of the Belsen Concentration Camp, as well as Dachau and Auschwitz, but they refused to believe what they saw. They said it was Churchill propaganda.

Grace was asked how the POWs she worked with were treated.

I don't know anything about their living conditions, and I don't think any of the girls did as they were so far away. So we had absolutely no contact with any of the prisoners other than working with them. It was very strict; you didn't want contact with them. This was your enemy. It was strange.

Social life for the WTC varied with their location—whether they were close enough to a town or whether they were isolated in the highland woods.

Well, we did make our own social life. We had a girl there who was very musical. She had some experience before the war entertaining and what have you. She got up a concert party and put on a show for the locals. Oh, it must have been awful! I shudder each time I think of it. Very occasionally, we got an invitation to a dance, maybe miles away. The army, the Royal Engineers it was, invited us. If there was no lorry available, nobody to drive you, you had it! You didn't go! The highlight of our week was going into Brechin, which was a small country town and we could go in and have something to eat. That was it! I don't know, there was always life about, always people, lots of girls.

I saw a side of life I had never experienced before, the open air, the fresh air. My family lived near the Clyde; you can imagine, the shipbuilders, the shipyards where they did the building—a completely different environment. Completely! You had blackouts and bombings. It was awful! I learned to appreciate the countryside. My husband and I used to do a lot of walking; walking around Perthshire and the hills. I think maybe I learned that—to appreciate the countryside!

Grace's final quote succinctly tells it all:

We had older men in charge who resented us. They didn't like us being there maybe because we were female, you know, the old Scottish attitude to women: They can't do men's work, BUT WE DID! (Armit: Kinross, Scotland, April 23, 2011)

Grace Armit (far right) felling trees with her WTC mates

Ina Brash

I was called up late 1942 and chose the Timber Corps when I could nae get in the service. I went in January of 1943, be time I had gone through all the interviews and medicals and all the rest. They took us tae Brechin in Angus. There was a lodge, Shanford Lodge. It was a huge building. We were trained there; we didn't live in the lodge. At least I didn't. We lived in huts, wooden huts you know! We had a few weeks of training; how to wield a four and half pound axe and a six foot saw. You know there was no mechanization then. Then after that our training was over, we were all sent to different camps. I was sent to two miles outside of Aviemore, tae a camp called Pityoulish Camp. It used tae be an army camp and had just been vacated by the army. All it was, was wooden huts, just army wooden huts. Another hut a bit away was for ablutions. But the toilet was just a hole in the ground with a box over it. Water was cold. If you wanted hot water, you had to fill the boiler and stand and wait 'til it heated up or someone else would take your water! That's what we had at first, but we never thought anything about it. It was all town girls. There were a few country girls, but most of them were town girls. We just got on wae it!

I was just cutting at first. We were taken to different spots—tae wherever they wanted cut. We either had tae walk there, well if it was a distance they would take us on a lorry— on the back of a lorry. Then later on, I was measuring. There was somebody that went around checking trees for the order they were looking for. They might be looking for pit props; there was a certain gauge of tree that they used for pit props—narrow for the pits. But for the likes of sleepers, they could be big ones because they went to the sawmill to be cut for whatever size was required. That's what I did—I was the measurer.

Ina stayed at Pityoulish Camp for about a year dealing with the hardness of winter and the environment of the camp, but doing her duty as best she could and "getting on wae it!" Then a major shift came for her and her mates. The old army camp closed but was replaced by a gift from Lady Seafield—the family lodge!

A well-known family, the Seafields lived near Grantown-on-Spey. Lady Seafield was very supportive of the WTC and gave over her lodge to use as a campsite. It was in a little place called Dulnain Bridge about three miles from Grantown-on-Spey. Of course it was wonderful. We had toilets and baths and everything. It was a big improvement. I was there until '46 felling the trees and snedding them. We worked hard; you know it was hard work. You had to cut down the tree then you had to sned it which was taking the branches off, and then you had to cut it to the size asked for and then you had to load it. Sometimes you had to load it into a pile where a lorry would come up and then you had to load it onto the lorry. And count, counting the props that went on the lorry cause of different orders: the pits or the railways. You had to count what was being sent. It was hard work, but the food was reasonable. We got a ration of sugar which was just a beaker and you kept it beside you, took it to the table, your ration of jam, you got that as well and you ate it or looked after it, and the meals were fine for me. You got soup perhaps, and a pudding. Other days, it would be meat and a pudding. You never got three meals; it was always two each day. We got in the morning a reasonable breakfast and then we made up our own lunch. We had butter of course, made our own sandwich with probably cheese or sometimes meat. We took our own sandwich to the woods with us, this was our lunch. When we came home at night, there was usually this dinner with two courses.

The women at Dulnain Bridge did enjoy themselves too! They were all young girls, excited to be doing what they were doing but also looking for adventure and fun!

The first camp, we were just two miles from Aviemore and so we could walk to town. There wasn't too much going on but there was always a wee dance or something like that for there were soldiers about. When we moved on to Dulnain Bridge, we were three miles from Grantown-on-Spey and there was always somebody with a truck that would drive us to town. On Saturday, we worked until twelve o'clock but the afternoons were free so we normally went into Grantown-on-Spey on Saturday afternoon. There are quite a few shops; it's a nice wee town. We would go and have our tea at MacKays in the square and then go to the pictures. And when we came out of the pictures, there was always a dance. There was a hotel there which is still there and a huge hall, just a hut of a thing, but it was huge and every Saturday night there was a dance! It was packed between the locals and the few soldiers that might be about and all the forestrys. The Canadians were nearby in their own camp at Bota Gardens. They were good at coming and taking the girls to their camp and there would be a dance with a band. I didn't go too much to those as I was too fat. I wisnae grotesque, but wisnae comfortable either. So I did nae go to many of the dances.

Ina was nineteen when she joined the WTC and twenty three when she came out in 1946! She experienced times she has never forgotten, met other young women who gave of themselves as did she and, although understated, has fierceness about the lack of recognition for the Scottish Women's Timber Corps. When asked, what the most meaningful part of her war experience was, she responded:

The war came on and you had to do your bit; that was what I did. In a way, we didn't get anything. We didn't get any recognition, pensions, or anything like that. Nobody knew anything about us. For many, many years any time I mentioned anything about my time in the WTC, they'd never heard of us. So it is more or less forgotten about for years—until the statue in Aberfoyle commemorating the Women's Timber Corps was established. That statue was the first thing, brought it to the fore! (Brash: Glasgow, Scotland, June 2, 2011)

Ina Brash in WTC uniform and working in the Highlands

There were eighty thousand British women in the Women's Land Army—Scots, Welsh, and English women. Of the six thousand women in the Women's Timber Corps, 4,900 were Scots, and the remaining were Welsh and English. There has been abundant publicity regarding the WLA: books, films, TV series, and articles. These women deserved these accolades but so did the WTC Warriors!

Rosalind Elder

Rosalind was sixteen when she decided she wanted to volunteer for service. This was in 1942, when the Brits were desperate and realized they needed the help of their women. Rosalind was living with her aunt at the time as her father had recently passed away. Her mother had died when she was four years old leaving Rosalind and her three siblings orphans.

My father had died and I had to find something. I tried to get into the Air Force because I had a sister in the WAAF. I tried to get in, but they asked me for my birth certificate and of course I couldn't produce it for you had to be seventeen and half. I was only sixteen! So I went and shopped around to all the different services to see which one would take me. I always lied and said I was seventeen and half, you see. The only one that would take me without asking for a birth certificate was the Timber Corps. So I joined right away and I thought now I am all set! But oh what a shock it was when I got there to see how things were going to be, living in a little wooden hut—with none of the comforts of living in Glasgow in 1942. Glasgow was a big city and was quite modern for an industrial city. We had lovely parks; we had museums, and art galleries and everything you could wish for. But up in the North of Scotland, we lost all that. We were stuck in the woods. Most of us were Glasgow girls—and Edinburgh. But we got along fine with each other, yes we did!

Rosalind's training began at the Shanford Lodge in Brechin where most of the young girls trained for the WTC. She moved on to the Advie Camp in Morayshire where she learned how to work with horses. She honed her skills and became known as the "horse woman." Because of her competence with horses, Rosalind was moved to various other camps to train others and fill in where there was a shortage. She was stationed in Grantown-on-Spey and then to Carrbridge. As the war wound down Rosalind was moved to Inverchaolain Lodge, Argyllshire, and finished up in 1946. During the four years serving her country, Rosalind experienced diverse situations, attitudes, standards—and learned what it meant to be in the WTC. She not only honed her skills as a "horse woman," but became a strong advocate for the rights of the women serving in the WTC. She has some strong, harsh words on their behalf!

I was a horse woman! I worked with horses and I had the only promotion that was possible. I was a leader girl. I got five shillings a week more than the other girls. I also worked on my own with a horse. The other girls worked in groups, most of them were fellers, crosscutters, and loaders—loading the wagons onto railway cars. But I worked with horses and I trained a few other girls to work with horses. But when I got to be seventeen and half, I thought this is enough of being in the Timber Corps. I want to go into the Air Force. I went to a recruiting office and joined the WAAF and they accepted me because I had a sister in the WAAF and because I was an orphan. When I informed the Timber Corps I was leaving to go into the WAAF, they said "Oh no, you can't. You are doing war work and you are more valued to us here than you are in the Air Force!" And so I wasn't allowed to leave. That was very annoying—we couldn't just walk off the job! Some did manage to get out, but I don't know how they did, but they did!

Staying in the WTC was not a bad thing. I quite enjoyed the work. I enjoyed being outdoors in the sunshine, working in the forest, the beautiful smell of trees—the lovely smell of the resin, the pine trees. It was beautiful in the summertime, but it's not always summertime in the Highlands. We had some cold days, and you would be freezing out there in the rain with your Wellington boots. We didn't have the equipment, the clothing that young people have today with the nylon parkas and all that. We just had woolen things and they got wet and it was miserable. Then of course we were out in the woods working all day. I pulled sixty trees a day. Some of the jobs I did were very dangerous. Like trees that were felled then fell into the gulley—a big hole. Then they asked me to go into the gulley and tie a chain around the tree and tie it around the horse. The horse was up atop, of course, but I had to get me and the horse out of the way as fast as possible before the tree would come skidding around. I had quite a few accidents but nothing serious, thank God!

Rosalind goes on to talk about the dangers of their work, the lack of care for those injured and the lack of compensation to cover the costs of those injuries.

Vera, my best friend in the Corps, was tying a chain on a swing bar attached to the horse, and the horse moved, and the chain gripped her fingers and she lost half of her middle finger in her right hand. Well, I heard her screaming. We got her in a taxicab to take her to the nearest cottage hospital in Grantown-on-Spey. They patched it up and she came back to the camp and then she was allowed to go home for a few days. No compensation, no nothing! She came back to the camp after she was home for a few days—she had no mother, no one to take care of her, so she came back to camp. I took care of her. Before I left in the morning, I'd fix her up and then again when I came back later in the day. She was right handed so she was quite disabled. She was a great pianist, too, and typist. Typing was her occupation in civilian life. If she had been a veteran, she would have received care and compensation. It wasn't fair! We were told when we joined up that we were equal to the women who joined the army, air force, and naval services. We had the Canadian Forestry Corp and Newfoundland Forestry Unit working in the Highlands felling trees. The Newfoundlanders were civilians. They didn't have a uniform at all but they were veterans according to Canada. They were treated as veterans. We had the uniforms and we were subject to all sorts of rules like, we had to ask for a pass to go anywhere. When we got our pay, we lined up to get our pay just like you would in the army, but then, we would have to go to another desk where they took most of that money for your upkeep, food, and lodging. It was crazy. Absolutely crazy! We were left with what we were told was pocket money. It was dreadful what little we earned and how much they took from us!

Rosalind had a good friend, Bonnie Macadam, who worked in the Shanford Lodge, the training camp in Brechin that all the WTC girls passed through. Bonnie stayed at Brechin for her time in the WTC instructing the new trainees. She saw many things and became another strong advocate for the girls in the WTC.

Bonnie Macadam saw several girls lose their lives during training at Shanford Lodge. She said they walked in the wrong direction—walked under the tree that was falling during the training. She had great concern for the young, innocent girls that joined up. Bonnie was very active and concerned during and after the war. She and I worked together in the later years, before we got our "Badge of Honour" from the Queen in 2009. We were fighting for recognition of all the girls in the WTC. Bonnie was constantly bringing it to the fore to get information out to people about the Timber Corps and the Land Army as well. She died just before the badge was awarded. There was a man, John Scott of Glasgow, who was younger than us, who tried to bring the work of the WTC to the attention of the authorities. But it was the Forestry Commissioner, James MacDougal, who really got the badge for us! He started the fundraising from the Forestry Commission. The first money went toward the badges, but it wasn't the badge I was after. I was after status for veterans! The girls over there, a whole lot of them have physical problems because of the work they did. Arthritis, which can be age related, but also related to the work they did, and other different things that could have been helped had they been veterans. It doesn't matter for me, being here in Canada—we have good health coverage and my husband is a Veteran in any case.

Rosalind Elder is the epitome of advocacy and fighting for what is right. She did what she had to do for her country and at the same time cared about the young women she worked with throughout her service and beyond. When asked: "What was the best thing about her work during the war?" She said:

Winning the war! We knew we had to win that war. I worked with German POWs and Italian POWs. I worked with them in the forestry and they were so sure that they were going to win the war. Definitely! When one young man, a Luftwaffe pilot, said to some of us that the first thing he was going to do was to shoot us all, I thought, what a nerve, and I said, "Well that won't happen." The German said, "In my country, we don't have women doing this kind of work, only in Russia do they do this." I said, "That's why we are going to win the war! Women in Britain will do this job. Willingly!"
(Elder: British Columbia, Canada, March 2011)

Chrissie Morrison

Chrissie Morrison was my first interviewee for this book. We spoke in her apartment in Glasgow, October 2009. Mrs. Morrison was on her own, still going strong at age eighty seven. She had some difficulty remembering details but was able to give some highlights of the two years spent in the Women's Timber Corps. Mrs. Morrison was a true Glaswegian with a very strong brogue.

I joined up in 1941, after women were asked to register for jobs. I thought, I could be a Lumberjill so I joined up. Ma sister was joining up tae. She went as a cook so I thought I could work outside. We were sent to Glen Etive which was near Glen Coe. After being in Glasgow most of ma life, this was very, very different—mountains everywhere. There were about thirty to forty girls at the camp. We used tae cut wood for railroad sleepers then stack them for the Lorries that picked them up. When it rained—aye and it rained aw the time— we had tae lay tree bark over the muddy trail then cover it wae sawdust so the Lorries could get tae Ballachulish then tae Oban for the boats.

Another job we had tae do was burn the tops off the trees tae kill the midges. They were bloody awful, some of us could nae stand them! The work was very hard and ye were dirty awe the time. Some of the Glasgow girls only lasted a few weeks then they went hame tae Glasgow. Other Glasgow girls loved being in the mountains. They even went hiking on the weekends. What I liked aboot being in the mountains was ye missed the bombings in Glasgow; ye didn't know there was a war on! And I used tae go tae Oban for a weekend sometimes. I liked that! It gave ye a break!

The food wisnae so bad—as ma sister was the cook, but we had tae pay about two pounds a week for room and board. So it was good tae go to Oban for a weekend and enjoy yerself and have a good meal. We also had a dance once a month. A couple of the fellas had accordions and violins making some guid music for us tae sing and dance tae. All in all it wis nae sae bad! The best thing of all wis all the guid friends ye made.

After almost two years, I left the WTC, and joined NAAFI—the air force division. I wis sent tae the Isle of Tiree and worked in the canteens taking care of all the soldiers that stopped by. I wore a uniform and worked three shifts: 10–11, 1–3, and 6:30–10:00 p.m. I wis there for six years and the best part about it wis, I was indoors all the time! (Morrison: Glasgow, Scotland, October 12, 2009)

Chrissie Morrison in her
Air Force Division of NAAFI uniform

Isabella "Tibbie" Scotland

Against her father's wishes, Tibbie volunteered for the Timber Corps in 1941 when she was seventeen. The eldest daughter of ten siblings, six boys and four girls, Tibbie was the second oldest and felt she had no say in her life.

I was at home. I had been ill because I had looked after my grandmother, well, she had Alzheimer's! They took me away from school tae look after her. Mind ye, I was fourteen, but that's what they did in those days. I lived with her for two years until she died. But I was with her every day, all day looking after her. My life had been controlled for so long it was time tae do what I wanted so I joined up. I volunteered for the Timber Corps.

The training started in Garmouth—that's the place that I come from. It's right in the mouth of the river Spey. We learned to fell the trees, take all the branches off, and then you had to peel the bark off because the forests that we were in had been burned so it was getting black bark on it. This was the kind of job we had tae do. Peeling the bark off was called snedding—that's it! That's what we did. After about a year in Garmouth, the boss came and asked for volunteers to open a new school, a training center. ParkHouse it was called down in Aberdeenshire. What did I do? Put ma hand up! The boss, Mr. MacLean, turned to me and said, "It's no good if you put your hand up, your father won't let you go!" So the second in command, he turned round and he said, "Mr. MacLean you asked for volunteers, you got one!" Mr. MacLean knew ma dad but they were not supposed to get into our private lives and the second in command reminded him of that! So off I wis tae ParkHouse!

When I got tae ParkHouse, we were nae long there when the government took over. The Women's Timber Corps it became and we had to have uniforms, which we had to pay for. We always had to pay; the huts we paid for, too. We had a lot to pay for; so much was taken off our salaries every week we got paid. Course in those days, it didn't seem to bother us. It was just a case that you accepted it all.

Tibbie was slowly, but surely finding her way. She thrived on her independence, making clear, confident decisions for herself. As her experience in the WTC increased, she began to discover the real

Tibbie, the self-assured Tibbie, the Tibbie who had a clearer aware-ness and acceptance of herself.

I stayed at ParkHouse for a while then I went tae Camp Garloghy near Keene, it was Aberdeen way. I worked out there for a while and then this gentleman came there for acquisi-tion. That's the side of forestry where you measure the woods, calculating how many cubic feet you are going to get out of one wood. So he came and asked for somebody. The boss said I could go! There were two other girls, three of us went, and we lived in the lap of luxury. We went down to Stone Haven where the woods were. We were living in the guest house get-ting well fed, well looked after, it was lovely! We had that for about three weeks. We got a good salary while we were there too. It was them that paid us. Our job was to measure stand-ing timber and I seemed to be good at calculating. The boss would say to me, "Tell me how many cubic feet in this one?" And I would look at it and tell him. "How do you do that?" he said. I said, "I don't know how it happens, it just comes to me. That's exactly what it is." So when the thing finished, he came to me and said: "I would like to be your boss and have you come to the acquisition side of it for you seem to know a lot." I told him when I was in school, I was able to give answers to math questions very quickly and they wouldn't believe me. The teacher would ask me, "How did you get that?" Once, I got the strap for giving the right answer so quickly. They didn't believe me that I knew it. They thought I copied it from someone. But there was naebody to copy off because naebody wrote answers down. The headmaster apologized afterward. He said he was sorry but that I had a "funny mind." But that was me; there was just something there, a brain like a computer sometimes.

When we got back to the camp, he asked the boss at Garloghy about me coming to work for him. The boss said, "You're not getting her. She is a good worker. I don't want to let her go." That way I lost the job and I was really cut about it. This is really me, this is me on to something I could do the rest of my life. I could be doing things like that! I was really angry at him. So angry that when a notification came from headquarters in Aberdeen about an opening at a driving school in ParkHouse, what did I do? I volunteered for it and was accepted! I was there for three months and then moved to my last camp over by the Loch.

At the driving school, we learned how to drive a Bedford and Ford Lorries. They were big Lorries. We had to carry the wood. You had to get your lorry loaded up and then had to go to certain places—like the side of the Holy Loch to a factory to deliver the wood. The first time I had gone up there, I was coming back through Dunoon. The boss, he was kind of worried, watching to see if I was okay, for it was a long journey and the first time on my own. I didnae see him but I got home. He told me he was waiting in Dunoon to see if I was coming, but he saw the lorry and knew I was okay. After my three months at driving school, I got shifted over to Lochgoilhead in Argyle. I didnae drive over there. It was back to the woods! It was mostly millwork we had there.

Tibbie moved around quite a bit ending up in two more camps before she was released in 1945. Tibbie saw herself as a "big person," becoming stronger with the work in the Timber Corps thus she gained a reputation as a good worker and was therefore called upon to do the really hard work in many of the camps. Unfortunately, Tibbie paid dearly for those years of pulling, lifting, and hauling heavy loads. It took its toll on her body. She began to have problems with her back which eventually affected her ability to walk.

The doctor told me about three years ago that he could never understand my back, the way it was. He said I had a back as if I was carrying bags of coal and heavy loads all the time. He asked me, "What did you do?" I told him about working in the forestry during the war. He had never heard of it. And I said, "Well, that's what I did!" "Well this is where all your troubles come from," he said. They had discovered something in my spine, something displaced, and that's what brought it on, the work I did! But also, I fell in 1970. I was coming off my patio and my heel slipped as I was coming off and I fell back the way. I broke my arm, and dislocated my shoulder, broke my pelvis in three places, falling over this bit in my back. Now I have trouble walking but I still get around. I still like to travel like coming tae see the Queen. I wid nae miss that!

I asked Tibbie if she felt she had contributed to the war effort.

Yes, well I did! All of a sudden, I really seemed to realize it! I'll tell you what it was. It was when the bombing started. And it actually affected us up north. Besides where I lived, my parents lived near an airport and of course that was the things they were targeting. Then in Aberdeen, there was the harbor, so we had them coming over trying to bomb. You know they did bomb Aberdeen, and when you are in the midst of it like that, you realize that's what you were really there for. Because the war meant nothing to me. You knew there was a war on but it wisnae at your doorstep. But when it came to ma doorstep, I began to realize that I am doing something for they needed this wood that we worked very hard tae get. Pit props in particular was one of the things and then there were coffins, telegraph poles, and all the different things they needed for the war and that there wisnae any men.

When asked, what the one thing she would like the readers to know about her experience in the Timber Corps—Tibbie gave this heartfelt response:

I'd really like to explain to them how much we did and got so little gratitude at the finish. That is the one thing that hurt us most! You came out, even in the village where I came from, everyone was having homecoming parties but we weren't included. We weren't appreciated. The ATS were coming out, getting uniforms, getting coupons, and got money. We got nothing! Nothing at all! That's why the memorial at Aberfoyle meant so much to us. Mr. MacDougall said to me the other day, "Great days, isn't it? Very touching to see that you did this for us." The young people of today like my doctor didn't know the Timber Corps existed. My daughter and I have been involved in so many things to try and get the Timber Corps noticed. So to wait until this time in my life, we are made famous—going to the Queen and the memorial at Aberfoyle, things like that. So many have shown appreciation since this happened. People understand what we did. It was hard; there is no getting away from that. It was hard work but good company! (Scotland: Edinburgh, Scotland, May 25, 2011)

Tibbie Scotland (second from left)
hauling wood with WTC mates

Mary Weir

Mary began working when she was seventeen in the office of a Glasgow cooperative until she was called up in 1942. Mary had many opportunities to choose from but she was pretty clear about what she wanted to do. She was also fortunate in where she had her first Timber Corps experience.

I was called up at nineteen. I got my calling up papers and I didn't know what to do. We got a choice of the ATS, WAAFS, WRNS, the Land Army, but the Timber Corps was just being formed then, in 1942. I went in in August of '42. You could also turn to munitions or nursing, but I wasn't interested. My father was keen that I would go to the nurs-

ing, but I didn't want to go into nursing. I thought about the Women's Land Army. I liked gardening. So it was the Land Army I had to go to. I waited to see where I would be sent. In between times, this Timber firm went into Kilfinan which is in Argyllshire and my sister lived there. I was visiting my sister and met Jack and Madelyn MacDonald, the owners of the company that supplied the equipment for timber felling. My sister told them I was in the Women's Land Army that I had been called up. Jack says, "We could apply for her." So they applied for me and I got there and got to stay with my sister. I was there for fourteen months. The first job I had, along with six other girls, was tae dig ditches to drain the water off the road because the tractors were sticking in the mud. Can you imagine that—us being asked to go and dig a ditch?

Mary had a variety of jobs to do working with the Timber firm. The girls worked alongside the men, like their assistants, sometimes doing cleanup work and other times doing work she never imagined she would do. This was Mary's training ground, where she learned just how much she was capable of, preparing her for the work at other camps.

I was asked if I would go to the sawmill and be a tailsman to the sawmiller. Which I did! There were two saws with a man on each: David and Jimmy. David took the bark off the trees and pushed it over to our side and we had to make it into planks. That was when we were daeing big trees, but then you had to stop because the saws needed sharpening and there was a whole day to do that so you had to go and do other things, like: clear the sawdust away, stack the planks that come off, and then ye had a day where you went with the men to load the lorry and take the timber to Arrochar Station which was fifty-five miles away from where we were. We went over this old road just west of Loch Lomond with a hair pin bend. I used to get out of the cab and walk round because I was a bit scared. We were on our way to load the wood on the train. Thank goodness, we didnae drive. The fellas did all the driving. But we did have to load the trucks. Aye, we had to load them. You always had to see that we had put chains round them to make sure they widnae roll off. I remember one night we were very late in coming back and the driver was very tired and we ran in tae a ditch six miles from home and he could nae get it out. He couldn't get the truck out and we had tae walk. It was one o'clock in the morning before we got home. Of course they were all frantic wondering where we were.

Working at Kilfinan, we were working for the Magolin family—the father and his three sons. The girls all had their jobs to do. There was quite a lot of men, of course. There was no felling in that job for us because it was all men that were woodcutters. We worked with the horsemen working in the woods. When they felled the trees, the horses had to go in and take them out to be loaded on the lorry. We had to go do that. What we did was, we rolled all the trees together into a chain and then it was hooked onto what they call a swingle tree and it was hooked onto that. The horses pulled it out down to the loading bay. And then it was loaded onto the pole wagon, which was like a tractor, and we pulled it up onto the main road, and then it was loaded onto the lorries and from there taken to the station.

After fourteen months, there was no more wood to cut down in the Kilfinan area so the Timber firm moved to Pitlochry taking Mary and three of the other girls with them: Rae, Faye, and Mickie.

So then we went to Pitlochry. At Pitlochry, there was nae sawmill. So it was then I had tae learn to fell! So Rae and I, Rae with Lawrence, that's a fella from the borders, and I went with Jimmy. They had felled and were wood cutters. We had tae work with them for maybe six weeks, learning how to do it. Which is, you lay in the tree, cut a mouth in it on the side it's going to fall, and then you saw from the back down. The saws that we had, they weren't mechanical, they were just hand saws and they had handles that come off if they get stuck, so you could pull them through. We were supposed to fell about ten a day, but I don't think we ever managed that—more like six a day, depending on the size of the girth of the tree. It depended

71

on the weather a lot, tae. The weather in Pitlochry, in the winter, was quite bad! I had an incident where I stayed with the gamekeeper and his wife and it was good. I got all the rabbit I could eat plus venison, grouse, and pheasant. Although there was rationing, we got all those things up there! But then one day, I remember going to my work and it just was a complete blizzard, a whiteout, you know? I came down and I thought I wisnae going to make it. It was so bad, it went for me, I couldn't get a breath. I thought, I'm not going to make this. I got to this wall and went over the wall. It was just like that! As though somebody had cut the wind off. I could breathe again. When I got over the wall, the gamekeeper from the other estate was coming toward me and he shouted, "Mary, come and see this." And I said, "What is it?" And it was a wild cat he'd shot. He had been looking for it for a while and it had been going for his grouse and pheasants. He had it over his shoulder and it was just like a tiger, only it was gray with big teeth. I'll never forget that!

Mary talked about the wonderful people she met and the good relationships that developed over time. Sixty-five years later, Mary is still in touch with many of them.

Rae and the two other girls, the sisters, were all Jewish girls. We all worked together. Rae and I worked often together. I remember one day in the woods she says to me "Oh, I'm hungry, come on and we'll have our lunch." Anyway we sat down to have our lunch and I opened up the box and I said, Oh! You can't eat this Rae. She says, "Why?" and I say, "It's ham." Rae says, "If I don't eat it, I'll starve. I need to eat something." So she ate it! Well recently—we still keep in touch—she says tae me. "Remember the day when I said I need to eat the ham? I'll always remember that, Mary, because I spoke to my sister about it and she said you've just got to do these things, its wartime, it's rationing. You've just got to do it!" So that was Rae!

A few years ago, a book was brought out. Timber it was called and Hugh MacDonald, one of the MacDonald brothers, got in touch with me after the book was published. I hadn't heard from him since the war. He says tae me, "You know, it's amazing, do you remember, Mary, the time we got the row for loading the pole wagon and it collapsed? I remember it fine, you know something went wrong, it was underneath and it collapsed. But the boss wisnae very pleased because it took a long time to get this going again." He and I remembered that day very well. Hugh said tae me that day, "Mary, I'm tired and you're tired, come on we'll go home, you get on Peter's back." Peter was the horse and I got on the back of the horse and he walked me home. Now my sister's house was on the shore, and we went along singing, "I've got Spurs that Jingle, Jangle, Jingle." Hugh and I had a great laugh that day he called!

One day, two men were down at the station with a load, afterward they came up tae where Jimmy Helham and I were felling away in the woods. So they came up and said, "We met Alan Weir down there, do you know him?" Jimmy says, "Oh, aye, I know Alan." "No, I don't know him," says I. "Oh, sure you're bound tae know him. He comes from Millhouse, that's the next village tae Kilfinan." I say, "I knew Peter Weir, but no, that's his cousin." They said, "He's working in Ballachulish, him and another fella. They're electricians." And two years later, I met Alan in Tighnabruaich and married him!

Mary was in Pitlochry a little over a year then was sent to a Timber Corps camp in Inverchaolain, Argyllshire in 1944, and remained there until she was released in 1946.

When I went to Inverchaolain, it was a camp. It was a felling camp, but it was a camp. It was a shooting lodge we lived in which was very good. I mean it was very good. Some of the girls had it really bad—the cold weather and awe that, and the huts they were staying in. There was about twenty odd girls and there were men, tae. Most of the men there were conscientious objectors. They were sent there to work in the woods. It was because they were so lacking in wood for the mines in particular. That's what people don't know. The Timber Corps was formed in 1942 especially for the wood that was so desperately needed. When the war first started, the men had to go to fight and there wasn't enough men. So the mines were closing because there wasn't enough pit props for them. But its nae just the pit props we needed. We needed wood for telegraph poles, for fire arms, for the huts, for coffins, and for railway sleepers. Some of that wood even went tae the Maginot Line! Not many people know that either.

So felling, it was for me for a while, but not too long after I was there the boss—a very good man—said tae me, "I think you should do the measuring, Mary, because I think you are quite good at figures." So I had to measure the length and girth of the wood cut. I was sent to measure especially when they were loading onto the boat at Inverchaolain. I had to measure and take a note of all the stuff that went on. You know how much they were getting? Fourpence three farthings a cubic foot. I can remember that to this day! I reckon it would be about ten pounds for a cubic foot now for the wood.

Mary finished her time in the Timber Corps in Inverchaolain filled with fond memories, wonderful friends, some hard times, but always positive outcomes. She has an awe-inspiring story to tell about felling a tree:

It wisnae just cutting the tree! There was something lovely about watching a tree falling. I canna explain it really, you know when you saw it just falling down, and you knew that you had planned it to fall there, you know? You couldn't do it willy nilly. You had them sort of here and there, you had to have them like so, that one fell there and that one fell here but then you had to leave a space in between so one between could fall. I always think back on it, when I think on a tree falling down, it was a lovely thing tae see, you know?

And at war's end—a very special memory:

The last day of the war, someone came, a lady driver, came running up to us all in the woods, "The war is finished, the war's finished!" Of course, we all ran away down into her lorry and went way along to Hopper's Pier and we danced there the whole night. And the lights came on in Rothesay. We were looking across to Rothesay and that's something I'll never forget. It was so exciting. The war wis finished!

I asked Mary if her experiences in the Timber Corps changed her in any way and how that affected her.

I lived at home with my parents and my father was very strict, you didn't get much freedom, he'd say "You be in at nine o'clock!" In the Timber Corps, you could go out to a dance, stay out for as long as ye liked. When I came back in 1946, it just seemed to be the same. Nothing changed. We saw things differently, though. We wanted tae work, the rations were still there, and we needed to work. Could nae get our jobs back, mind ye. The job I had in the office was filled with somebody else, and I had to go and work in the shop. I worked at the cash desk. Don't know what they call it today. It was really bookkeeping. I think we just went back to the usual. The usual way of living!

My final question to Mary was: What would you like the readers to know about your experience?

Well, I think just, to think about us, think about what we gave up to go and do that! Because, you know, I think a funny thing happened when I was going to London to see the Queen. When we went into Central Station I use a wheelchair and we were sitting, Lyndsay and I (Lyndsay is Mary's daughter). Lyndsay's friend had come in and a lady porter came over, and she said, "Could I help you?" and Lyndsay said, "No, it's all right! I think we're okay." The porter says, "You'll need a ramp to get on the train," and she went and she turned to me and said, "Are you going for a few days to London?"

I said, well not really. Then Lyndsay said, "She's actually going to Buckingham Palace." Porter says, "Oh, why are you going to Buckingham Palace?" and she was very interested in why I was going to Buckingham Palace. Then she went away and she came back, this time with her boss, Mr. Duncan. He says, "I believe you are going to Buckingham Palace? Well, I've upgraded you to first class." Very nice! So he took us up and arranged it all and took our stuff into the train and took me

*to my place and sat me down. I said, thank you very much!
And he says "No, thank you very much for what you did for
us!" Twice that was said to me—again when I was down in
London. The driver we had took us from the hotel to the Opera
House for our lunch, then to the Palace, brought us back to
our hotel, then took us on a tour of London. When it was
over Lyndsay, wanted to tip him and he said, "No, no way!"
I said, "Well thank you very much." He said, "No, thank
you for what you did for us!" That meant something to me.
Because nobody ever said, "We'll you did it!"* (Weir: Glasgow,
Scotland, March 11, 2010)

Mary Weir in WTC uniform

These are the women of the Timber Corps—the Lumberjills!
They had amazing stories to tell in their own special way. Of the six
women interviewed, five were from Glasgow, and one a country girl,
Tibbie Scotland. Five were still living in Scotland and one had immigrated to Canada, Rosalind Elder. All were married with children and
some with grandchildren. They went on with their lives but never
forgot what they did and how well they did it! We owe them a lot!

WTC Memorial in Aberfoyle, Scotland

CHAPTER 7
A GREAT LEVELER OF PEOPLE

The following interviews are with Scottish women I met through family friends or through the Daughters of Scotia (DOS). One was interviewed in her home in Tampa, FL, USA—Anne Donlan; two were interviewed in Scotland—Cathy Clark and Lucy Findley Burns; and the remainder were interviewed in California, USA in their homes or by telephone. With the exception of Clark and Burns, the women had immigrated to the United States within a few years after WWII ended—beginning a new life with dramatic changes.

Lucy Findlay Burns

I volunteered for the ATS in '42 when I was seventeen. My mother didnae want me tae go but she was fed up aboot me nagging tae go so she signed the paper so I could go. She was a widow and ma two brothers were away. My eldest brother was in the regular army and my other brother was conscripted and he hated every minute of it. He was a Dunkirk veteran. It was a very, very bad time. There were nae jobs. Work was very, very scarce. So I joined up along with many of my friends, but we were scattered all over. I was the only one that went up to the Cameron Barracks at Inverness. Now there was an experience! You speak about being cold. You've never felt cold like this in all your life. Inverness is really exposed and the barracks are really cold. They're made of solid pink granite and inside its still solid pink granite. There was nae insulation and the damp seeped through. It was a long dormitory with thirty-two beds, three or four feet between each bed. There was a wee stove over at the very end of this long room. It was like an old-fashioned hospital ward. And you were only allowed one shovel of coal

*which ye kept for the evening tae try and keep yerself warm—
but that did nae work so we froze! We even tried keeping our
clothes on tae try and keep warm. Then at six o'clock in the
morning—just when you were kind of dropping off tae sleep—
this infernal bagpiper started up. Ye could have shot him at six
o'clock on a cold January morning. It was January, February,
when I joined. Oh My God It Was Cold!*

Lucy continues with her description of her three weeks of training in Inverness, one of the most northern camps in Scotland—a
beautiful spot, but obviously not in the middle of winter.

*It was perishing cold and the food, of course during the
war, was pathetic! One night, for tea, you would get a sardine,
the next night you would get a smidgen of cheese. It wasn't very
much. Then we were being jammed with these TB injections
which were really sore and you were laid low for forty-eight
hours. After that, you had blisters on your feet. Your feet full
of chilblains and stick them into these new shoes as "hard as
charity." All your feet were blistered. It was the most miserable,
miserable three weeks I've ever spent in my entire life!*

"Hard as charity," an incredible and telling expression, comes
from the Calvinistic era of Scotland where you were taught to be
hard working and independent. To accept charity for any reason
would be the hardest thing anyone could imagine themselves doing.
This was definitely a "hard" lesson to learn, but learned they did! The
Scots are well-known for their independent nature and taking on any
kind of work. This theme is illustrated throughout the book in the
stories told by the Scottish women.

After the three weeks of training in Inverness, Lucy was stationed in Manchester, England working as a store clerk—or as officially called, Quartermaster Clerkess. She spent two and half years in
Manchester with short postings at other locations.

*I was down in London for a wee while but that was just
a month's posting. It was quite an experience with bombs flying. The Doodle Bugs were pretty frightening. They were like
rockets. I remember being told, "Its only a bomb, you'll get used
tae it." When ye heard the bomb ye lay doon, once it stopped*

that's where it was going to land. So they were quite frightening—Doodle Bugs! Of course there were plenty of bombs in Manchester as well and we had barrage balloons just at the end of the site we were on. The Air Force girls struggled with the barrage balloons—trying to keep them afloat and protecting the area from bombs. Whereas we were army but it was just a sport field we were billeted on, nothing at all on it. We did nae have much protection—living in these corrugated iron huts. And the food was just as bad as it was in training camp. Because of the rations that's all they could feed you on. There was nae sugar available. It was awful. But we had some good times too. We'd go to the local church army dance, make a fool of ourselves. There were lots of Americans. Of course any girls who went with Americans, well we know what you're after! You know, lay themselves down for a pair of nylon stockings. Some of us didn't want anything to do with them. There were different nights for the white Americans and the black Americans. I said to the rector, "What's the big idea, what's going on?" He said, "Oh they'd kill one another." That's how it was. It was apartheid at its worst and it was true, they would have. Blacks were never allowed out with the whites and the whites never allowed out wi' the blacks.

I was in Manchester for two -and half years. You know I think I enjoyed my life then. We grumbled like fury, but there was nothing really to grumble about. Especially once we went to a unit. We were a lot more comfortable than we'd been in training. That was the worst! But the best part was just the company and the friendship. We were all in the same boat, nobody had any more than anyone else. It was a great leveler of people. I learned an awful lot. I grew up, I suppose.

When I asked Lucy what she thought about women taking over the jobs the men left behind for military service, she responded:

It was something that had to be done. We didn't think anything of it. But I think it did open up the world to women and of course women were just men's chattels before that, weren't they?

Lucy's response to what she would like the readers of the book to learn from her experience was:

It took me out of my home environment into education. I used the army like I would have if I went to university. I became independent and I think it did a lot for me. I was a gregarious person. I was meeting people, different people from different walks of life and it gave me an insight into what real life was like. (Burns: Aberdeen, Scotland, March 10, 2010)

Cathy Clark

In 1939, Cathy, the eldest of four sisters was thirteen, and was not conscripted until she was seventeen and a half in 1945. She chose the Women's Land Army. Scotland had its own Women's Land Army with the Women's Timber Corps being a part of it. Although I was able to interview six WTC members, Cathy is the only interviewee who served in the WLA. Thus, making her experience not only unique and exciting, but also a powerful rendition of what the women in the Land Army had to endure in order to provide the necessary food for the country.

I went first to East Kilbride working the farm. It was close tae ma home in Glasgow. You could see our house from the farm. So I milked the cows, did the dairy dishes, chased after turkeys at night when they got up in the trees. There was just six cows on the farm, there was no byre man, and there was only two land girls. It had its good side in that we had milk and a wee milk route, delivering milk in Burnside and Glasgow, which wisnae far away. But we weren't getting fed. The farmer and his wife chained smoked while they filled the milk bottles by hand. We got nothing to eat until that was all done, but they had already had their breakfast while we were working in the byre, milking the cows by hand. So we put our coats on one day and said, "That's it!"

Cathy was soon stationed in a contrasting, happier environment, a farm in Ayrshire, Scotland.

I went to Ochiltree in Ayrshire and that had no electricity. It had Tilley lamps, a lamp that we had tae pump. It had twenty cows in the byre at a time. It had turkeys and a pig, you name it. It had everything. There wis only one Land Girl! Me! There were two byre men and a German POW and the ploughman. That was hard work. But I got fed on the farm! When I was at East Kilbride farm, I got a weekend off once a month from Saturday lunchtime and I had to be back by Sunday evening. In Ayrshire, I got a weekend once a fortnight and we stopped in the middle of the milking on a Friday and I did nae come back until the Sunday evening. I had quite a bit to travel to come home but I could come home with eggs and butter, and a sheep's head for the soup! I never got things like that on the farm that was nearer tae home. It was so much better there in Ayrshire. I'd go out in the fields and there was always somebody else. I wasn't on my own. There was always a man there to help. I mean, I would come tae a great big turnip and wouldn't be able to get it oot because the frost was in the ground. And the German, Klaus Titman wis his name, would shout, "Leave it, I'll get it!"

Cathy goes on to tell a fascinating chronicle of Klaus Titman's journey to Britain.

Klaus was captured in Libya in North Africa and taken to America. He was in Arizona in a POW camp. Whenever anybody broke out of the POW camp in America, they never went looking for them because Arizona is a desert. But the ones that managed to get back tae the camp, they shipped them over here tae the UK. Well, him and four lads broke out but only two got back. The others must have died in the desert. So they were brought over here and Klaus ended up at the farm I went tae. He and a lot of other German POWs were called "displaced persons" because they came from the part of Germany that was now in the Russian Zone. Klaus knew he could never return to Germany. So he like many German prisoners stayed on after the war. They stayed in Scotland.

I asked Cathy: "What was the best thing she got out of being in the Land Army?"

Well, see up here in Scotland, it was different. Mostly down in England, they were trained first and then went to the farms. We just went straight on the farm and you just picked up as you went along. The boss would say, "You need tae do this, Girlie." They'd give me a stool and I had tae go milk the cows by hand. It was a good hard morning's work. I wis learning on the job! When I turned up at Ochiltree's, Mr Sloan, the boss says: "I knew they were sending us wains." But I got on wi' the family. They were a great family, the two byre men and the ploughman and Klaus Titman, they were great to work wae. Not only that, I could go out to the wee town of Curnock where all the Land Girls in the area would meet at this wee restaurant and have a good time together. I enjoyed myself and we just took ourselves to a lot of change. (Clark: Glasgow, Scotland, October 10, 2009)

Cathy was in the Women's Land Army for almost two years. The war was over but she continued in service to her country by joining NAAFI in 1947. In 1948 she was stationed in Germany and while attending a gathering in the NAAFI Club, she met "her hubby"—the young man who became her husband. She certainly did take herself to some wondrous changes.

Cathy Clark in Woman's Land Army uniform

Violet Healey

In December of 2009, I was in the Sacramento, California, area visiting my sister Peggy. We put together a list of Scottish women who had served in WWII and who are now living in California. These groups of women were either friends of Mary Scharosch's mother or were reached through the Daughters of Scotia organization. I was scheduled to either interview them face-to-face or via telephone. The following interview was with eighty-nine-year-old Violet Healey via telephone on December 17, 2009.

My sister and I were both conscripted. I was nineteen and she was sixteen—so we both had to join the war brigade. I was taken to Penicuik, which is outside of Edinburgh. I was trained there as a PBX telephone operator. That was what I was doing. My sister was trained to be a truck driver. Would you believe that? She was sixteen years old and that's what she did! Well I did the telephone thing. You know, pass on messages through the connection to the big board. Whoever was calling we connect them to whoever they wanted to talk to. These messages all had to do with the camp at Penicuik. It was quite interesting though sometimes I had to work all night. I did nae like that very much.

Violet had some difficulty remembering how long she stayed at Penicuik but she did recall being transferred to Leadenhall Street in London.

I know I got moved. I was in London working in Leadenhall Street next to St. Paul's Cathedral. I was doing office work and stuff, and of course the bombs were falling so I had a vision of that. Oh, every night they would come dropping bombs and set every place on fire. Thank God I didn't live anyplace near there. But I could see the fires and, oh, the people that were killed. It was terrible!

These were difficult memories for Violet for they brought up other horrible war recollections.

I remember at the beginning of the war, we had no idea what was going to happen. I lived in Paisley, Scotland, close to the Clyde, near Renfrew. I remember one day there was a terrible commotion. Evidently, the Germans found out there was petroleum, big huge tanks of gas and stuff along the River Clyde. They flew up and set fire tae it. They damaged a convent that was next to where I lived, so that's how we saw the war started. I had another experience. I was on leave down in Falmouth for a little rest, and I heard the bombers coming. They whistle when they come down sometimes. So I was in the house and I had an awful feeling maybe the bomb was going to hit me or around me. So I got out and went to a concrete shelter. We all had these concrete shelters out in the back or other places that you had to go to when there was an alarm. So I went there and right enough the house next door to me got hit. I was out in the concrete shelter and I just got blown off my feet. Oh, it was terrible, the dust and all the noise—but I was okay! But ye never really knew. Sometimes, you were at the theatre and all of a sudden the alarms would go off. You didn't know if you were going to get hit in the theatre or so many other things where hundreds of people were killed. Oh, it was terrible. I'll never forget that. Whenever the alarm came off you hoped you were in a position to be out of the damage, you know?

Violet's time in the service was brought to a drastic halt!

After a while at Leadenhall Street, it ended up badly for me cause I was coughing up blood. I had to go to the hospital. I had a spot in my lung so they sent me home for six months recuperation and that was the end of it for me. I had to stay at home at Paisley and take medication and check in at the clinic every other day. Oh, I don't know what I had, TB or what? They couldn't tell. They just could see the spot on my lung. I had trouble breathing, coughing up blood. So that was the end of it. I felt badly that I had to stay home. Here's my sister still plugging away. But I did go through a lot. I must admit, misery and those bombs dropping all the time. Some of the planes got shot down and the pilots parachuted out. Of course they had to be caught. There were all those prisoners around too. Give me strength!!!

Anyway, it was not all bad. When I was still in London, my sister Margaret came into town as part of her job. When we got together, we went to an USO dance. We were both dancing with people so Margaret met a very nice young man. He was an American pilot and eventually they got married. Isn't that wonderful? Of course, I did the same thing. So that's how we ended up here. In America! We were both GI war brides if that's what you like to call us. But ma marriage didn't last long. I wisnae happy. I couldn't live the way he lived. His mother did nae like me and that was the end of us. I just left! Not long after I left, I decided to visit my sister in Kansas City, Missouri. Margaret and I had a lovely time together. One night, we went to the Palladium to hear Sarah Vaughn singing. While she and I were sitting talking, this very good looking young man came over and asked me to dance. That's how I met my husband, my new husband! I was married tae him for fifty years. He died in 2001, so I have been a widower ever since. I miss the heck out of that man. We were so close and we had a wonderful life!

I asked Violet: "What is the one thing you would like the readers of the book to know about your experiences during the war?"

Well, at the time, there is a feeling that you have to help your country and that helps you to go through it all and do the best you can. The Germans wanted to take over our country. We didn't want them to so that was the reason we were quite happy to sacrifice more or less and do what we had to do.
(Healey: Sacramento, California, December, 17, 2009)

One of the most critical areas of need for the war effort was munitions. As predicted by Sir William Beverage, one and a half million British women would be required to work in munitions alone. This was indeed the case! Hundreds of thousands of women worked in Scottish munitions factories—many in the Glasgow area. The Rolls Royce factory in Hillington built Merlin engines for Spitfires and Lancaster bombers. Ten thousand women worked in that factory alone! The Dalbeattie explosives factory had 2,200 workers, two thousand of which were women. One of the oldest factories in Glasgow was the Singer Sewing Machine Company which produced millions of sewing machines over the years, but also produced munitions for the war effort utilizing the skills of thousands of women. There was a torpedo factory in Greenock. The Beardmore Plants in Parkhead, Mossend, Grant's Mill—Mile End, Cordonald in Paisley produced seventy-three war ships, one huundred tanks, 516 aircraft, and eight-hundred-plus Howitzers. Glasgow/Clydebank area became the "capital" of munitions production and the Scottish women were the primary producers. Working in munitions was a dangerous job—dealing with high explosives and irritant chemicals which caused allergic reactions and in some cases loss of limbs or lives. Margaret Clark and Peggy Tomkins are excellent examples of the Scottish women who exposed themselves to the perilous job of munitions.

Margaret Clark

Margaret responded to my inquiry in the Daughters of Scotia newsletter as she had served in munitions during WWII and wished to tell her story. As Margaret was now living in Dearborn, Michigan, we set up a telephone interview for December 8, 2009.

> I was sixteen at the beginning of the war and had a job in the Templeton's Carpet Factory. But I soon lost it. They told us about two weeks before the Nazis invasion of Poland that we should start looking for another job because our looms could not be converted into blankets. So immediately my aunt told me about a job in the grocery trade. Of course I went straight into the grocery job. The men began leaving—being called up every day. Before you know it, I'm the only female manageress and quickly got into being boss. They took every man we had at this job. I had been there for a few years when I got called up. It was 1942 and I was nineteen when I had to go into munitions. Our job was tae make Howitzer shells. It was all done in this place called Stewarts and Lloyds, a steel tube manufacturer. They actually made the steel tubes and we made them in tae Howitzer shells. We worked in the machine shop where half of us were women, but as the war went on, there were more and more women doing the work. Then there was the

other thing—ah was an Air Raid Warden. I had tae put out incendiary bombs as part of that job. I went around Glasgow with these guys—we called them policemen but they weren't policemen. They were called "specials," so we used to have tae go in flat roofed buildings where they had pails of sand and a wee thing like a rake. Then we'd take the incendiary bomb that we found and put it in the pail of sand, cover it with the sand and it didn't go off! I didn't know what it did, but it did nae go off. We did the same thing around the tenements as well— putting out the incendiary bombs.

Living and working in Glasgow, especially as an ARW, during the war, gave Margaret enormous insight into what was actually going on in her environment and how it all was impacting the people.

I lived in Glasgow and my job as an air raid warden kept me close tae the tenements where my family, my grandma, and my great aunt lived. Now we were very close tae Clydebank and John Brown's Shipyard—that's where they made the Queen Elizabeth, the Queen Mary, and all those big ships. So when the Nazis were bombing us, John Brown's Shipyard was really the target. But they kept missing there and they kept bombing us. We got very little sleep. I know London was really hard hit, but then again we were very hard hit tae because we were kept awake with the "POM, POM" shells. They were our shells. We liked that when we heard our shells 'cause they were after the Nazis bombers. That's what the Nazis were trying to get. They weren't interested in Glasgow. They were trying to get the shipyards. They never hit the shipyards, so that was really a blessing.

We worked as hard as anybody as an ARW. When I was on duty, I had three closes where I had to take care of all the people there. I had my aunt in one building and in the next close my Grandma. Then in the next close, was a lady that was blind, so I made sure she was awe right. I used tae go tae ma Grandma's and help her during the blackout. She wisnae able to pull the blind down; so I would stay with her for a while during the blackouts and get everything in order.

Margaret tells a thrilling tale of how scary and traumatic war times were, and yet, when looking back, can seem fortuitous and oddly comical.

The Germans were trying to get the Power Station. Now the Power Station provided electricity for all over Scotland, and it happened to be a block from where my mother lived. My mother didn't have an air raid shelter so she used to go over to my girlfriend's sister's home and stay with her. Well, there had been a terrible loud explosion. Everyone thought the Power Station had been blown up. I thought, "Oh, my God, my mother!" So I'm trying to get to my mother but you weren't allowed to walk in the street during an air raid. You were supposed to be in a shelter. So the guy I was walking with, walked me to the next shelter and handed me over to the warden, then to the next warden until I got close tae my mother's house. When I finally got there, I found out the bombing had missed the Power Station, but had taken out a beautiful red brick building right next to it. A good friend of mine had been there at the time. Her boyfriend had just left her but had run back when he heard the noise. He found her standing there, touched her, and she fell. It had taken all the air out of her. She was completely dead! I ran into my mother's house. No mother. Where is she? What happened? I see all that happened was the blast blew my mother's teapot onto my mother's bed, spilling water all over it. Very soon, my mother returns from my friend's house. My sister had been with her tae. They were both all right. It was a scare, I'll tell you! These were the things that happened, some of them unthinkable, some of them quite funny. I mean, later on, when you think about it, the only thing that happened to our mother was she got her bed wet!

Margaret went through a lot—a multitude of stress, extreme pressure, and crucial adjustments in her life. I asked: "How did her war experiences change her?"

Well, you realized you could almost do anything if you wanted to do it. I mean, I fixed electric switches. You hadnae any men, so what else could you do? You had to take care of things yourself. It made you more independent. I can honestly and truly say, it made a big difference to me as far as being independent is concerned. I was the type of person that just did things. My husband was a medical director of a steel mill before he died. I was the one that packed the cases. I was the one that packed the car. Then I took the car and picked him up. It never was a case of: "Oh, I couldn't do that!" I was never a shrinking violet! I could always do everything. Well, I'm eighty-seven and I take care of my own house. I do my own washing. I'm going blind, but I'll never go blind. I'm positive I won't go blind. I've got macular degeneration. "It's my age," I said to the doctor. He said, "You're taking it well." I said, "If I cried, would it help?" He said, "No." So I said to him: "Okay, you've told me its age related, so, I either go on living and doing the best I can or I die!" He says: "Well, that's a good attitude to have."

Having an independent nature has been important to Margaret as she has been a widow for twenty-eight years. She takes care of herself as well as being good to others. Having a love of life, enjoying every moment she can, Margaret travels to places she and her husband relished and took pleasure in. She often attends the Daughters of Scotia conferences and delights in visiting gambling casinos in Las Vegas.

As we were finishing up our conversation, I asked Margaret: "What was the one thing you would like the readers of the book to know about your experience during the war?"

If you're dedicated, if you love your country, you would do as much as you could. Well, when I was asked to do some-thing, which I was asked to do a lot of times, it kinda went against the grain. But you had to do it, and you did it and you didn't complain. I was dedicated to the country, to my country. I was, and I won't ever let anybody say anything bad about Scotland! Ever! (Clark: Dearborn, Michigan, December 8, 2009)

Peggy Tompkins

> *I lived in Edinburgh and used tae work in printing
> which was only a few minutes away from my house. When I
> got called up, my mother told me, "No decent girl is joining
> the services." They had a bad reputation back then when I was
> growing up. So when I got called up, I went into munitions.
> I was about seventeen or eighteen and I had to go to Glasgow
> to train for about six weeks. It wasnae too bad because they
> showed you what to do and you just did it! The thing that was
> horrible was I used to live a short way from my work, whereas
> we had to get up and take a bus, go across town to finally get
> tae the training place. Eight of us went up there and stayed
> for the week, Monday through Friday and came home on the
> weekend. I wasn't a morning person so that was hard for me to
> travel all the way to Glasgow.*
>
> *After the six weeks of training, we got sent to Ferranti's
> and sometimes had to stay overnight just in case they dropped
> these incendiary bombs. That's the type they just drop down and
> sputter away and catch fire. So we had to be careful that the
> Germans going over didn't drop any of these kinds of bombs.
> We had to stay overnight, go home, and come back to work the
> next day. When we slept there, a gang of us and people took
> turns in watching. You know you could tell the difference in
> the engines of the planes, ours or the Germans. So it was a kind
> of exciting time.*

During WWII, Ferranti's was a major manufacturer and supplier of electronics, fuses, and valves for Britain. In 1943, they opened a factory in Crewe Toll, Edinburgh, which manufactured Gyro Gunsights for Spitfire aircraft. They employed thousands of Scots, mainly women.

> *Edinburgh never got bombed that much, just the out-
> skirts, but you never knew. When we heard the air raid siren,
> we'd get all kinda excited, get down to the shelter that we were
> designated to and stay till the sirens stopped. Of course there
> was the blackout. It was pitch black and it was very hard to
> see much except you knew your way around a bit, you know*

you lived there all your life. The best times were when we went dancing and there was an air raid on. You could nae get out in the street because they wanted you to stay inside off the streets—out of the way! Anyway, we loved it at that time because we got to stay until the air raid siren cleared off. This way we got to dance longer. That was kinda the fun part of it.

Peggy and her coworkers were very much like any other young teenagers of the times; wanting to live their lives, do exciting things, and have fun. But these were extraordinary times and it meant performing in an unprecedented manner. And this they did. They "just got on wae it!"

Wae the air raid sirens going, it was kinda exciting. You'd get down to your shelter and be safe. Then it got to be kinda old after so long and that you just got used to it. You know being real brave and stuff like that! Our job at Ferranti's was good. We did our job—we did what we had tae do! The one thing that we all grumbled about was it was on the other side of town. You had tae catch a street car, and then a bus and it took forever to get there. And it seemed like it was always raining in the morning. But the best part was the people. People's spirits were up. We were all very close. They used to make jokes about the war—as if it was really somewhere else. We didnae get bombed much. At times we didnae really know there was a war on. I had three sisters and I didn't have anybody real close in the service. So we didn't really have to worry an awful lot. (Tompkins: Sacramento, California, December 24, 2009)

Anne Donlin

Anne, who now lives in Tampa, FL, was interviewed on February 20, 2010, about the war years and her time in the ATS.

My twin brother was in the RAF and I wanted to go into the RAF too, which would have meant the WAAFs for me. But when I was conscripted in 1943 at age eighteen, my papers came for the army first, so I had to go. In WWI, it was called the Women's Auxiliary Army Corps (WAAC) but then in '38, it became the Auxiliary Territorial Service, so I was really going into the ATS. I went to regular training in Yorkshire and from there I went to North Wales. I did my training to learn to drive there. I drove cars, ambulances, and what we called three ton trucks. Over here, I think they are called eight wheelers. It was a big truck! Sometimes I would get this big truck, but I always had to have a guy to help. I was at a camp in Inverness for a while. We stayed at this big house; actually it was a castle, where they used to have hooks hanging with meat and stuff. Some of the guys went out shooting—hunting, I guess, which gave us great rations. We even had chocolate and candies too. We had Italian and German POWs working with us. They were there to help me and the other women. One of them made me a pair of sandal things with rope and another made an ashtray from a piece of tin. We all got along very well. It was nice.

Anne learned how to play the piano as a young girl and became quite proficient. During the war, her skills as a pianist and her love of performing provoked a great deal of attention her way, making her life in the ATS a rewarding experience. Anne has continued to perform, teach, and take joy in playing the piano. In fact, at the time of this interview, at age eighty-four, she was the pianist for three organizations—the Daughters of Scotia being one of them.

Well, I started off as a private! And then this guy heard about me playing the piano at our company dances. He was a major and he got in touch with me and said he wanted me to be in a concert party he was having. It had people attending from all over. It was quite the big thing. This major asked me what did I do and I said, "I am in charge of the ration store." I had to get all the food for the people—males and females—at two different camps. The next thing I knew I was called up in front of the biggie to tell me I got two stripes, not one, two! So that was fine. I was getting more money too. And then we were sent down to Perth and I was made a sergeant there. I did office work. I was the bookkeeper for that. I was still playing the piano. Wherever there was a piano, I was playing! Even in canteens, I used to go and play. I enjoyed my life in the army. I really did!

Anne went through a most unusual experience while serving in the war but she realized that even in painful times, working in the ATS proved to be comforting and uplifting.

> *I was about nineteen or twenty and in my unit by that time. I woke up one morning and I didn't feel well at all. I was miserable. I wanted my mommy, although it was always my daddy that I was greetin' for when I was home sick. I wished I were home! I went on sick parade and was sent to this place that we had to go to, like a hospital. They told me I had German measles. They said to me, "Does your face always look like that?" I said, "Like what?" and she said, "Look in the mirror!" Oh, my God, no! I was covered with these spots. I never realized it was on my face. I was in there for quite bitty and made friends with a wee WRN. We were way up in Inverness. It wasn't so bad after all.*

Throughout Britain, there was a continuous attempt to allow a "break time" to the people in service—men and women. These came in the form of company dances, concerts, Whist Drives, and many other types of entertainment for the troops and women in service. Whist is a British card game and a Whist Drive is a social gathering where Whist is played, four to a table. The winners of each hand move to different tables to play losers of previous hands. Anne tells a touching but telling tale of one of her experiences at a Whist Drive.

> *I was at this Whist Drive and there was a young lassie there about my age. She was Land Army. One of the people organizing the event said to me, "I'm surprised there aren't more service people here. You are the only one." I said, "No, I'm not the only one. That young lady there, she is in the Land Army. That's army, just as much army as I am army!"*

It is obvious that Anne Donlin had a strong spirit. She has always been supportive of all of the women who served, standing up for them and herself! She met and married a Glaswegian lad during the war—the love of her life! When asked what the most memorable experience she had during the war, her reply was to the point! *Meeting my husband, of course!* (Donlin: Tampa, Florida, February 18, 2010)

Jeanne Shepherd

Jeanne Shepherd was ninety-seven years old when I interviewed her in her home in Sacramento, CA on December 20, 2009. She was twenty-seven when the war started and had a three-month-old daughter which prevented her from serving in the war. Her husband was called up on September 3, 1939, the day the war began. He was stationed in England for one year, allowed a three-day pass to go home, and then transferred to Egypt where he stayed for five years. Jeanne professes she didn't do anything to help out during the war. She takes for granted the role she did play!

When my husband was sent to Egypt, he was gone for five years. No phone calls in those days. He did write letters, but I did nae get many because they were all censored and he wrote about the same thing all the time. So he did nae write very much. It was hard, but the war was on! I was on my own and just had to do what I could. I mean I had a three-month-old baby. I had tae make the best of it. I could nae do any job for the war service. I could nae do anything.

We lived in Glasgow near Clydebank and there wis bombers flying over us awe the time—every night! Ye never knew when a bomb was going tae hit ye. I remember the noise, hearing them coming over during the night. I could nae get down tae the shelter because there wis a stone stair going down and I could nae go down there in the dark wi the baby. So we'd just go under the bed. The best we could do! I think it was the shipyards what they were really after. The German bombers were trying to get the ships and factories and my house was pretty near the harbor.

My daughter Irene, to this day, hates a noise for she was about six before the war was over. She knew how to be scared. The air raid wardens would come around if they heard the least little peep or there was a light coming from your windae. They would come rapping at the door tae let you know ye had to keep quiet and close your curtain. It was mostly during the night that the bombers came—seldom in the daytime, mostly during the night when it was cold, wet, and dark. The sounds

*were terrible, the planes, the noise, and the thud of the air-
planes. The noise of the plane alone would scare you, then the
sirens on top of that. Irene is seventy now and she says she hates
noises because it sticks with ye. It scared her a lot. Scared us all!*

Jeanne continues her reflections of her life in war torn Glasgow,
not only what she and her daughter endured, but also, how they pre-
vailed through thick and thin!

*Food was very scarce. Everything was rationed. You only
got maybe a piece of meat for a week and a bone to make soup.
You just had to make the best you could. Irene was allergic to a
lot of stuff and they would give the kids cod liver oil. Well, she's
allergic to fish, so she couldnae take the cod liver oil. Aye, it
could be hard at times. Ye didnae have yer husband in the first
place and there wisnae many places to go, really, 'til they went
to school. I walked tae school with her all the time because the
kids were scared to walk alone. I didnae do much during the
war. I thought my husband would get home but he never did,
for five solid years! It was just a case of looking after her and
my neighbor and us going to the park wae the kids and stuff
like that.*

*When ma husband came home, there was a bunch of
kids playing in the backyard and I said tae him, "Why didn't
you bring Irene up when you came?" He said, "I didn't know
which one was her." So I went down and got her. When she
saw him, she wouldn't have nothing to do wi' him. He was in
a khaki uniform and we didnae see many uniforms. She was
scared stiff o' him. Didn't want anything to do wi' him!*

After hearing Jeanne say a number of times that "she didnae do
anything during the war," I suggested that she did a lot! She did a lot
because her husband wasn't there and she had become dependent on
him after bearing a child. All of a sudden, she was on her own, raising
a child, running the household, and enduring the trauma of life in
war torn Glasgow. She answered with the following:

*You had to go downstairs for your coal and your sticks.
And the washing day, ye had tae go doon in the morning and
light yer fire, come back up, hae yer breakfast, go back doon*

and dae yer washing. So ye had to go up and doon the stairs and ye had to take the kid wi' ye. A days washing took a whole day. Then when ye hung them out, the rain came on, back you would go and doon for yer coal. The cellars were away doon and round the corner. I mean it was a tenement house I was in and I was in the middle floor. So there was a lot he would have done—taking the coals and sticks up for the fire and stuff like that.

My neighbor and I would go for walks in the afternoon. Take the two kids with us, stuff like that. So it was tough going. There's no doubt about it! Ye just had tae put up wi' it! We're lucky we got through. My husband was a bit better off than we were. He was in Egypt and dinae hear a bomb the whole time. We were getting it all the time.

One of the things that sustained Jeanne during these hard times was her passion for dancing. Fortunately for her, there were opportunities for her to attend Friday night dancing.

There wasnae a whole lot you could do. There wisnae too much went on in Glasgow. Most of the men were gone. It wasn't the same. Even when we tried to go to the dancing on a Friday, ye just danced wi' somebody, girls and that. When I just wanted to get out once and again I'd go tae Friday night dancing and my sister would take care of Irene. I always liked tae dance. I danced when I was a kid. I learned ballroom dancing and highland dancing. I used tae dance a lot in Scotland. My husband and I loved tae dance together. When we came tae America, I started teaching. My youngest, Myra, was a great wee highland dancer. I wis teaching her and one or two kids of the women in the DOS (Daughters of Scotia). When Myra got older, I started teaching a whole bunch. There was a crowd that wanted lessons for a group called the Bluebirds. Before ye knew it, I was teaching the granddaughters of the women in the DOS. I've been teaching dancing 'til I retired at age sixty-two.

I asked Jeanne what she would like the readers of the book to know about her experiences during the war.

Well, I would like them tae know what it really was like during the war. You know, when ye had tae hide under the bed when awe the bombers were flying overhead. When ye had tae walk yer kids tae school because they were scared. And that ye just had a little bit o' meat tae eat. We dinna hae too much tae eat during the war. Everything was rationed. Then your letters were censored, you couldnae say too much in your letters, you know what you wanted tae say. You never knew when a letter wis coming. Sometimes, ye didn't even get them. You couldnae get phone calls. If I did get a phone call, I had tae go up tae a certain place to get it. It wisnae easy. You couldnae relax very much. Ye always had something else tae think about!
(Shepherd: Sacramento, California, December 20,2009)

Jeanne Shepherd was not called up to serve her country in WWII, but she certainly kept the home fires burning. She had "tae keep on wae it," providing as safe a home as she could for her wee yin. She, like many of the Scottish women like her—courageous, dependable, tenacious, and undaunted—sustained their homeland for the men to return to.

CHAPTER 8
JUST GET ON WAE IT

Finding Scottish women who served their country during WWII was a daunting adventure, but also a mind altering experience. For in my quest to speak with these women, I realized most had passed on, but that they had left behind their grown children filled with amazing stories of their beloved mother. These are incredible tales, of not only what their mother did, but how it impacted them and influenced their lives, and in many cases, the lives of their children and grandchildren.

Jean Ferguson Caloz—daughter of Agnes "Nancy" Brown Ferguson:

Since I was born in 1935, the war years were my formative years as a youth and also affected my early teenage years. My father had joined the Royal Air Force in 1939. My mother, Nancy, went to work for the transportation department in Glasgow as a conductor on the trams—that's trolleys to you, Yanks! Her sister, my aunt Margaret, worked as a conductress—a "clippie" as they called them in those years, and my mom's other sister, Aunt Belle, was a warden in the ARP (Air Raid Police). Granny Brown took care of my sister Sadie and me when my mum was working. It is interesting to note that before the war, the women wore only dresses. But the war changed all of that. My mum and aunts wore slacks as part of their uniforms and that continued after the war. I believe that the necessity of working while the men were "away at war," made the women of Britain more independent. I know my mum and aunts continued to wear pants or trousers after the war, and even when they immigrated to America.

Jean depicts a heart wrenching time during the war when she was about seven or eight years old—when bombing Glasgow was the norm.

> *One evening, my aunt Belle showed up at Granny's house, very concerned. I was supposed to be asleep, sharing the same bed with Sadie in the alcove in the kitchen. However, I overheard the conversation. Apparently, there had been a night bombing raid in the area of Maryhill, where the depot that my mum worked out of was located. It was thought that the building had been hit, and it was not known if anyone had been injured or killed in the raid. Needless to say, I lay there under the covers, afraid to say anything, but sure that my mum had been killed. Thankfully, my mum arrived home about an hour later. She told us that she was on one of the last trams running that evening. They had just finished up and clocked out when the air raid siren blew. Since we lived fairly close to the depot by tram, she decided to chance it, and come straight home rather than seek an air raid shelter. However, she had to walk and it took about an hour. I still cry when I think of her running all the way home, not sure if we had suffered any bombing and if we were all okay. That decision probably saved her life.*

Jean tells an emotional saga of how the war impacted everyone, including the elderly. Although little recognition has been given to the women's role in WWII, even less acknowledgement and gratitude has been bestowed upon the elderly—the grannies and the grand-dads who contributed more than we can ever realize. Our Granny Brown was deaf and had been since her childhood, but even with a hearing disability, she lived in her own apartment in the same tenement building as Jean, Sadie, and their mother, Nancy. While Jean's mother was working on the trams, Granny Brown was holding the fort—keeping the children safe.

> *When the air raid sirens went off we would run down to the Air Raid Shelter, which was built in the middle of the street. The shelter was made of brick and had stairs leading down to it from the tenement building. Often, we were carried*

there in our nightgowns, wrapped in blankets. The residents had stocked the shelter with a stove and a teapot, and all the necessary items to nourish us, during, what sometimes lasted into the wee hours of the morning. I never felt afraid during those times as my mum and/or Granny were always with us. We knew other families, and invariably someone would begin to sing, and or course, we all joined in. Sometimes, my Aunt Belle, who was an Air Raid Warden, would be with us. She had a very funny rendition of the song, "A warden in the ARP," and often would sing it to us during the air raid. At some point, I would usually fall asleep on someone's lap until the whole thing was over, and then return to our apartment.

Toward the end of the war, I recall a visit that Granny and I made. I was probably about nine years old. I went along with Granny because of her hearing disability and to help her communicate if necessary. We were on our way to visit an old friend of Granny's. The previous day, there had been a very severe air raid, and she knew that the bombing had destroyed many buildings. When we arrived at the stop on the tram line, we walked for a few streets while Granny tried to get her bearings. Eventually, she stopped and just stood looking at a building, which had been demolished. She was crying, and then she turned to me and said, we should just go home. She had no idea if her friend was alive or dead. I realize now, that due to her disability, she was afraid or unable to make inquiries regarding her friend. I think that is when I realized the bombings were real, and that people were actually being killed.

I asked Jean what her feelings were about her mother's role in WWII and how that impacted her life. Her answer will tug at your heart and is indicative of just how inspiring the role the Scottish women played.

Mum stepped up and became head of the household while my dad served his country. Her dedication to our wee family seemed only natural to me at that time. She worked to support us, keeping us warm, safe and loved, at a very scary time for a young girl of five through ten years of age. Looking back on those years, I now realize what an extraordinary role she played. She had no choice but to keep the family together by putting on a pair of pants and becoming a conductor on the local trams. I am so proud and in awe of her. Like the "Rosie the Riveter" of the USA, she became one of the many thousands in a different kind of war, keeping the "home fires burning." Many years later, as a member of a professional women's group, I had to write a speech about the woman I admired most. I chose to write about my mum. Her bravery, tenacity, and love of family are what made me the woman I am today. I won an award for that speech, but no award could ever replace the love in my heart for my mother. Putting it in writing only made me understand after all those years, what she had done for us, her family.

How has that impacted my life? There are situations and experiences in all our lives when we have to make decisions, sometimes very difficult decisions. I believe that my mum instilled in us the courage to face those times and to know that I would make the right decisions. So many times I talked with my mum about those times in our lives. I had watched her go through serious problems all her life and seeing how she was challenged and how she handled them was a lesson to me when I needed to do the same. She was the "wind beneath my wings." She was that to me and more. I trust and hope that my children and grandchildren have recognized those same values in me, and can use them to help them over life's bumps. (Caloz: New Jersey, July 25, 2009)

Myra Cowan: daughter of Mary Brown

I interviewed eighty-year-old Myra Cowan in December of 2009 in Sacramento, California. The story that Myra depicts of the war years is quite representative of many of the British families of that time, but as a Scottish family living in Knightswood section of Glasgow during WWII, it depicts the dourest of times. Myra was only ten when the war began with an older sister and three younger siblings—one brother and four girls total. Her father joined up in the British Royal Navy and was assigned to the Fleet Air Arm (FAA), which is the aviation branch of the Royal Navy. Eventually, he was sent off to Egypt and served there for the duration of the war, leaving her mother, Mary, to keep her children safe and sound throughout the worst of times.

My Dad went to Egypt during the war and he was there for a good long time, probably about three years or so. I don't know exactly how long Dad was gone. We were young and we just knew he was gone! Our mom was with us. She was not involved in the war, but she had to get a job to keep us going and fed. She worked in a fish shop as a fishmonger. That part was good because we had fish to eat. That was more than most people had because of the rations. But there wasn't much fun going on especially when mom was out of the house at work. We kids were left by ourselves. Back then, a lot of kids were expected to help around the house, do the chores, and so on. We didn't have much of a childhood. I just remember feeling very unhappy. Day to day life was pretty dreary. Not much fun!

Living through the war years—1939 to 1945—Myra was age ten through sixteen—formative years, years that had a significant impact on her.

I remember the air raids in Glasgow and having the Anderson shelter in the backyard and having to go there on a regular basis. When the siren sounded, everyone collected their coats and blankets and went out to the air raid shelter. I lived two streets down from Bankhead School in Knightswood. That was bombed! They dropped a land mine upon the school. We had to go to another school after that. The bombing was at night so no one was in the school at the time. There were air raid wardens but I don't recall any of them getting hurt. Shortly after that bombing raid, we were evacuated to Prestwick. We were gone for a short period of time actually. We hated being there. Mom missed us and so we came back home quite soon, but we were split up. We were five, but she kept the baby home and we were separated when we went there. My younger sister, the one next to me, she was about a year younger. She and I were put with an older woman—single woman! Very spinster-

ish! She was set in her ways and being a spinster she was not used to having children, so we were put in our place and told to sit there. We didn't have much fun when we were there. I don't recall how far away my two siblings were as they were in a different place than us. We were probably gone only a few weeks when my mother brought us back home. We hadn't had any schooling so when we got back home, it was after one of the air raids, we got walking up toward the school we attended. We were walking up the hill to the school and you could see craters in the street where the bombs had dropped. That was exciting to us kids, I guess, at the time. We would stop and look at them all and ooh and ah. But fortunately, we weren't hurt, any of us. I don't recall that any of our immediate neighbors were hurt. But it was scary! Our school tried to help us deal with the air raids. They taught us how to get into the air raid shelters to duck down and cover ourselves. We called it "duck and cover." But they didn't talk about the war. They just helped us prepare for the air raids with the "duck and cover." I think they just wanted life to go on—life as usual for the kids.

The war years impacted Myra's mother with significant consequences to her and to her family. Known as a woman with a great sense of humor and joy of life, Mary loved to dance and be socially active. She missed her husband and the life they used to have, making the war years stressful and lonely.

The war years were hard on my mother, working every day, caring for five kids, and my father gone. She was lonely a lot of the time. I think that is why she found somebody else. She worked every day and it wasn't a fun job especially in Scotland. It was cold and with the shops windows open, you know where they used to display their food, she was always freezing. It wasn't a fun time for her at all. She wasn't happy. Too many things were missing. And all that responsibility, having to work and worry about us kids. We were mostly on our own. We were all in school, but then we came home to an empty house. We had a few relatives but they lived across town and they had their own lives. I'm sure that was a big strain on my mother, but I don't think us kids appreciated how much of a strain it was. Then there were the air raids and my mom trying to keep us safe. For all of us being in the Anderson shelters at night when the air raids were happening was the worst times, but also must have put a lot of stress on my mom – worrying about keeping us safe. Apart from that, we more or less accepted the day to day things as a way of life. We were sad; we missed our dad of course. We were happy when he came home but then the home situation was upset by that time. My mom was going to leave our father. It was a sad time for all of us.

In 1945, Myra was sixteen and working in an office as a typist—a skill she acquired from an unexpected opportunity resulting from her natural, innate kindness.

I went to a business school, and was there a short time. My girlfriend's mother and father sent me there and paid for my tuition so I could go. They were very appreciative as their daughter Margaret was alone and no one wanted to play with her. She was crippled and she couldn't get out to play. I spent a lot of time in their house, so they became dependent on me 'cause I spent so much time with her. They even took me on vacation with them to Largs. It was a wonderful thing they did for me, allowing me to go to business school where I learned shorthand, which I hated, but learning typing became an important asset for me. I became quite proficient which lead to good jobs later in my life.

With all the responsibilities in her early years, Myra grew up fast—working a steady, responsible job at sixteen, dating seriously by seventeen, and ready for marriage by eighteen.

I was dating a young Glaswegian and fell in love. We wanted to get married but some interference from his mother not only delayed the wedding but the location. His mother and his mother's sister were concerned about the people he was running around with in Glasgow. His aunt and uncle had a nice home in Sacramento, California. So old style, his mother shipped him off to somebody that would have him, his aunt—his mother's sister. So he came here and I followed a few months later. We went to Reno and got married, then came to live in Sacramento. We were married thirty-nine years and had three kids. My husband passed away in 1986 and my kids are grown with children of their own. My only daughter is in the Virgin Islands working; I have a son who is living in the Isle of Man with his wife; and my other son lives in Oklahoma with his wife and three kids. They all recently surprised me with a visit for my eightieth birthday. It was really great!

I asked Myra how the war had impacted her: "Was there anything in particular that might have changed you in any way or changed how you thought about things?" Her answer was so honest and sincere—a tribute to her integrity as a person.

I think I really appreciated what I had a lot more than the young people that I met when I came here, people my own age. I wasn't jealous of the things they had but just wondered how in the world they could have all these things when I was forced to live such a plain, simple life! Even here, we never made a lot of money, and so the kids started coming a year and half after we were married. We lived as we knew how to live back then. We didn't have a lot of fancy foods or rich surroundings. We were typically Scottish people, hardworking and trying to do the best we could. When I first came here, I went for a secretarial job at an insurance company having been to business school and learned typing. I've always been complimented on my skills so I did feel confident that I would do a good job. The fellow I worked for was an older man, probably old enough to be my father. He was very supportive of me and complimented me many times on my skills. He always made me feel good. When I became pregnant with my first child, being the Scottish girl that I was, I didn't go around talking about it. Obviously, I started to show a bit, not very much just a wee bit! I decided to tell my boss I was going to be leaving soon to have a baby. He said to me: "Myra, I've been waiting for you to tell me that!" It was funny at the time. Such a nice man!

I had a final question for Myra: "What would you want the readers of the book to know about your experiences during the war?"

As young children, we were scared to death—the noise, the commotion that was going on around us affected us greatly. I think the families that were left at home did a good job of taking care of one another. I can remember just good neighbors always there for you. They did it because they had to. It was the right thing to do. There was no other way to be. You had to help one another. I just think I have been very fortunate in my life since then. Coming from that kind of background, you appreciate simple things and that has been the story of my life. Never had a lot of expensive items; never had a lot of money to spend, but I think I accept that, simply because I wasn't leaving anything behind ever. It wasn't a big change for me when I came over here. The people were quite different because they hadn't come through what I had. I did leave all my family behind except for my mom. She eventually came to America too and she loved being here. She just loved being here. She joined the Daughters of Scotia (DOS) and soon had lots of friends. My mom had a great sense of humor and loved to share her laughs with her DOS mates. My mom used to do these skits with her friend Betty Connelly at the lodge entertaining the other lodge members. They played the part of two wee wifies having a blether as they sat around having tea. They would do their hair up in curlers, usually both wearing an old apron while cracking everyone up. She loved it and everyone loved her. All my sisters and brother stayed in Scotland and they are all gone now. I got to be eighty years old and they all died in their late sixties. But I am happy now. At the time I first came here, I wasn't happy. But I have had a good life since I came here. (Cowan: Sacramento, California, December 20, 2009)

Isobel "Ella" Todd MacDonald – daughter of Jean Brown Todd

Ella's mother—my aunt Jean, my mother's sister—was a remarkable woman; loving parent, hardworking, and a loyal Scot. She did whatever was necessary to not only care and provide for her children—all five of them—but do whatever was crucial and urgent for the war effort.

My father was called up before the war was announced because he was in the Territorial Army from his time fighting in the First World War. He shouldn't have been called up as he was forty-one years old and had five children, but he was because he was already a trained soldier. So he was off tae war leaving my mum wae the five kids. At first she was working in a factory getting way less pay than any man would get. Then she was able to get a job working at Glasgow Central Station as a rail porter because it was all females that was doing the men's jobs by that time. They didn't get the pay that the men got, but they got better pay than what they'd have gotten if they were working in a factory. They were doing the same job, but they didnae get the same pay as the men.

She began working in the stables looking after the horses as my father had a livery stable earlier in their marriage and my mother knew how to handle the horses, what and how to feed them, clean them, and care for them. She did nae do that for long for they could get a young boy to do that job, and they needed her to do other jobs more important like seeing the mail was put on the right trains and things like that. So my mum worked at Glasgow Central Train Station as a porter. At the time, all the parcels and goods went by railway. They came in and my mum had to pull this big wagon of goods and then load it all on the good's train. It was different back then. The goods trains are separate now—they are loaded into carriages or containers now. But back then, it was hard work. My mum hurt her wrist pulling this trolley thing along wi' all the goods and had tae wear a special bandage on her wrist to protect her. So my mum continued to do her job making sure the right parcels went to the right location. Things were being shipped from Glasgow to Inverness or Glasgow to Aberdeen, or whatever trains left Glasgow Central Station; my mum knew all the routes and what parcels went on where. She became a leading porter, which meant she managed the job, teaching others to do the work she had learned. This was entirely new to women as no women got jobs like that before the war.

My aunts also did jobs that no woman did before the war. My Aunt Belle was an Air Raid Warden and that was a man's job. She had tae go out at night during the blackout—it wis pitch black and she would have tae go up tae people's door and tell them tae close their blinds and put out the lights or they'd get reported. She was trying to protect them as the bombers could see the lights and then drop a bomb. So it was really serious work she was doing. Then there wi's my other two aunties, my aunt Nancy and my aunt Margaret, they were doing a man's job too. One was a conductress and the other one was a driver in the Trams. That was a first too, only men worked in the Trams before the war.

Belle Erwin, Air Raid Warden in Glasgow during war

Living through the perpetual air raids with the fear of being bombed was a continuous plight for Ella and her siblings. She talked about her apprehension regarding her father's orders to her mother. He was afraid of what the Germans would do to his family if they managed to take over Scotland so he told her mother to "turn on the gas and kill us all" if the Germans land in Glasgow. Ella couldn't get that message out of her mind, being forever vigilant during the air raids, listening for the sound of the gas being turned on. Ella never told her mother about her fears as she felt her mother had enough Herculean tasks of her own to manage. It was a horrific time for all, still impacting Ella to this day. But she has some positive memories of that time too.

One of the best memories I have about my war experiences was how helpful the people of Glasgow were to one another. The Glasgow people were always like that anyway, but during the war, everybody was like one big family. They looked out for each other especially where we lived where lots of people lived up in six closes. It was like a wee village. When we came back from the evacuation tae Glasgow, it was in the spring and it was dark when we got off the train. We were walking up Parliamentary Road and it was during the blackout. My mother had the five of us as we had already picked up my wee brother Robin as he was up at Maryhill St. with my sister Jean. So there was this man coming down the street carrying a torch (flashlight) and he had tae have it shaded so it did nae give off much light. He must have been going to work—the night shift. So the man says tae my mum, "Where are you going missus?" And she said, "We are going up tae 270 Parliamentary Road." He said, "I'll be late for work, but come on." He showed us all the way up, right up to the very door. I was so happy to be home.

When the war was finally finished, we had bonfire nights. For a while, every night we had a bonfire and everyone was going out and singing and dancing. We were all that happy the war was over. We had great times singing, a favorite pastime of the Glaswegians. On VE Day, there was a big rally down in St. George Square and my sister Margaret and I went down. Margaret and I were great pals as well as sisters so we went to celebrate and everyone was singing and having a jolly time. I lost my shoe and I only had one pair of shoes so I was really upset. I had to find it, but it was so crowded. The crowd was swaying back and forth and pulling us along with them. So I couldnae look for my shoe so I had tae go home with one shoe on. I went looking for it the next day and I found it— would you believe that! It was flattened like a pancake. I had tae put my foot into it to get it back into shape as this was all I had, this one pair of shoes. Clothes were rationed too, and you had to make things last.

As the war ended, increasing numbers of men were demobbed—coming home as late as 1946 expecting to return to the job they had before the war. Women were required to relinquish the work they not only had taken over, but had enhanced. It was time to go back to being a housewife! But things had changed—the men did get their jobs back, but to many it wasn't quite the same.

Although a lot of guys came back to their same jobs, it was not the same. The job was scaled down—different, you know? There was a lot of unhappy folk when they came back. In fact, they got a job women had done. I think that must have felt a bit demeaning to them. After all, in those days, a woman's place was in the home! But the war changed all that. Women didn't want to "just stay home and dae the washin' or knit cardigans and jumpers. They wanted tae work at a real job. There were more women in the job market by the fifties than ever before. And then there was a whole culture change. People started going abroad holidays that had never done before. People were getting more adventurous cause guys had traveled and seen places. Most folk had always just stayed in the same town and if they went to the seaside, it was for one week a year or something. It was mostly like that in Scotland for sixty percent were working class. (MacDonald: Northern Ireland, October 16, 2009)

There were definitely significant cultural changes in Scotland after WWII as Ella pointed out. Scotland as well as the rest of Britain had a difficult time recovering from the war. Rationing was still going on in the early '50's, jobs were fewer, and more people needed work. This cultural change brought on the great migration—increasing number of Scots and Brits immigrating to America, Australia, and Canada. Ella's parents never considered leaving their homeland, nor did Ella. Her love of Scotland has grown more fervent over the years. She married her love, Bob MacDonald, and had five children all of whom share their mother's love for their homeland, Scotland!

Learning how to be a kiltmaker, opened a whole new world for Ella. She and Bob began their own business, outfitting people worldwide in Scottish kilts—bringing a taste of Scotland to many. Ella passed away in 2010. Giving the strength and fortitude she learned from her mother to her children and grandchildren, Ella lives on through them, as they are now kiltmakers, perpetuating what their mother, grandmother, and great-grandmother stood for: An everlasting love of Scotland!

Stronach O'Neil – daughter of Elizabeth (Betty) O'Neil

I met Stronach quite accidently through a mutual friend who knew I was writing this book. Stronach was born in Scotland but has spent most of her life in Canada due to her mother marrying a Canadian serviceman during WWII. While visiting Florida in February of 2011, Stronach agreed to meet with me to talk about her mother's part in the role the Scottish women played during WWII. She described her mother with such love and admiration—giving an elaborate portrayal of the person she truly was. Betty O'Neil personifies what serving their country actually meant to the women of Scotland. Here is her story expressed eloquently by her daughter Stronach.

My mother grew up on the outskirts of a tiny fishing village, the rugged northeast shore of Scotland. She was a Highlander for sure. Life there was limited and her family was very, very poor. I think, however, that my mother always had a strong sense of adventure and zest for life; so when the war started, she joined the WAAF. I believe she did that to see the world, expand her horizons, and experience more than she could in such a small place.

My mom went through training in England. Here's this country woman with very limited experience, being taught to drive these huge transport lorries. I don't know if they were the equivalent of eighteen wheelers but they were enormous. I remember my mom talking about how really difficult it was to learn to drive them. Not only were they big, but also cumbersome with a standard transmission that required her to double clutch. She said that she would go to bed at night with that refrain running constantly through her head, "Clutch in, clutch out, clutch in together!"

She was stationed at an air force base in Banbury, England, during the war. It was a very active field with many aircraft and a radar station. Mom did a lot of driving with a wide variety of vehicles. In the large lorries, she transported anything and everything including supplies and troops from base camp out to the airfield and back. She also drove an ambulance. Often she spoke of feeling an adrenalin surge as the base siren heralded the arrival of "our planes" back from a mission; of rushing with the ambulance right up to the crippled airplanes as they careened onto the tarmac; and of racing injured and dying airmen to the hospital. I recall her speaking about how she really had learned to live in the moment because of the horrors she experienced while on ambulance detail. Sometimes, after they had transported badly injured air crew, it was necessary to clean body parts out of the ambulances—body parts that were those of men they knew somewhat; those of men that they had laughed and danced with; or most what was most difficult, men that they were close friends with. That was really, really hard.

Stronach's mom spent most of her war experiences in England where she endured, up close, the air raids and devastation of the continual bombing of London and the surroundings areas. Stronach relates two very different incidents that occurred during the ravaging bombing raids.

My Uncle George, my mom's brother, was in the Merchant Marines when his ship was torpedoed and exploded. He refused to leave the ship until all his men were off, resulting in his feet being burned down to the bare bones. As a result, he was awarded the St. Georges Cross for bravery. Mom, her sisters, and my grandmother all went to London to watch George receive his medal. During the ceremony, they had to hide under the tables in the hotel where the ceremony was taking place while the bombs were hailing down. The hotel was actually hit. What an irony! Looking back, it is surreal to me that this young woman, my mom, who is in her early twenties, in the heart of the war, wearing a gas mask, going to shelters in London—and that other young women were doing the same thing—going through all of this. It is amazing!

The rush to the shelters also happened at base camp. One day, Rennie—a good friend of mom's and about mom's age, rather "proper" and always wanting to look her best—was in the shower when the air raid siren went off. Soaking wet, with suds streaming down her face, she grabbed a towel and rushed out of the barracks to get to the air raid shelter. Once she was out of doors, she fully realized her predicament. She could not, in any stretch of the imagination, cover everything with her regulation—but very skimpy towel. She was not at all sure what to do, so she just kept moving the towel around, trying to conceal all her crucial private parts. My mom loved telling that story about Rennie.

I remember asking my mom what it was like during the war, if it was frightening. She said that there were times when they were afraid, but for most part, there was a sense of life as precious, as something to be lived moment by moment. So they tried to live life to the fullest, with lots of laughter, lots of friendships, and a real sense of bonding and intimacy created with others that in normal circumstances would probably not have happened.

Stronach describes her mom as someone who loved to tell funny stories. She always expressed herself in an entertaining way, taking from her life experiences its humorous side. Stronach gives an excellent example in the telling of a lorry incident her mother experienced during the war.

One day, my mom was transporting supplies from a distant depot to the base, when she passed a group of service men stranded on the side of the road. Their transport lorry had broken down and they were a long way from their base. Mom stopped; opened the flap in the rear of her lorry and they hauled themselves up into the back of the cargo hold. As soon as they were settled, she dropped the flap and climbed back into the driver's seat. After a considerable distance, she and her female co-driver badly needed to take a pee break. Totally forgetting that they had men in the back of the truck, they hopped off the truck; went to the back of it so that they would have privacy. They were squatting with their pants down around their ankles, when all of a sudden, there were all these hoots and hollers, screams and wolf whistles erupted. Still in their "compromised" position, they looked up to see a whole row of faces peering out from under the tail flap. The woman who was with my mom was really upset and ran crying to the front of the truck. Mom calmly finished peeing, stood up, hauled up her pants, saluted the men, got back in the truck, and drove away. She carried it off!!

Stronach's mother, Betty, came from a large family, and therefore, was not the only one who was conscripted. Her eldest sister, Christine, was a nurse who eventually became a nursing supervisor while stationed in London caring for civilian casualties as well as wounded military. Betty's younger sister, Jean, was also involved in the war. She managed to serve in the latter years working in a factory near Elgin.

My aunt Christine was this very capable woman, with a brusque, no nonsense approach to life, who worked her fingers to the bone. Underneath this tough exterior was a humorous and loving woman with a huge heart. But when she was in her professional garb, she laid down the law—absolutely! No one dared mess with Head Nurse Christine. I remember my mom talking about her sister's exceptionally high standards of cleanliness and care. It was critically important to her that people be cared for properly. Then there was my aunt Jean, the baby of the family and a young teenager when the war began. She was conscripted when she became of age and worked throughout the war in a factory in a neighboring town. Even before Aunt Jeannie was called up, she and my grandmother, like most women in their small village, were always doing what they could to support each other and the War effort.

One of the most significant events of WWII for Stronach was her mother meeting her father and how that event changed their lives.

The Royal Canadian Air Force (RCAF) had a group of men, part of an undercover radar operation, stationed on the same base as my mother. These Canadian men were considered to be "the exotics." My mother was especially interested in one somewhat reserved fellow. She did what she could to subtlely attract his attention. Part of my mom's job was bringing back supplies from town to the base, some of which was for the mess hall. She would bring food back for that area and surreptitiously set aside the really good treats, like muffins, and hide them on the transport seat, snuggled next to her body. As soon as she arrived back on the base, she would drive to a tree hidden behind the camouflaged radar building. A sharp pull on a string rigged to the "secret" tree rang a bell inside. On the signal, someone would sneak out and scurry back with the "hot" treats my mom quickly passed through the truck window. Apparently, over time, that someone was most often my father. Her strategy certainly worked.

Stronach's mom married the Canadian serviceman and lived in private married quarters until the end of the war. Stronach was born in 1945 and her father was shipped back to Canada. Betty returned to Scotland with her wee baby to be with her family. When Stronach was fourteen months old, in July of 1946, she and her mother sailed to Canada to meet her father and begin their new life. This was a life changing event for Betty, moving from her homeland to another world entirely. Stronach talks about the enormity of what her mother did as well as many other women who thought they met the man of their dreams and followed them to make a new life for themselves.

It was a life changing event. Huge horizons just opened up and I think about the sense of pride, optimism, trust, and the bravery of these women too. I imagine the amount of courage it must have taken for each of them in their own particular circumstances. I think about my mother, leaving her closely knit family—her clan to relocate from her tiny village to an unknown city in a vast country. I think about the fall-out from that trust as well. Countless numbers of women who left the known in their lives became war brides and came to Canada—some of them not knowing anything about these men. One of the things that stands out for me is the memory of my mother talking about these courageous women on board the ship, some with children, some without who arrived in Halifax, and there was no one there to greet them. The men they thought they had married were already married or for any number of reasons had absolutely no intentions of coming for them—ever. Many of the women were returned to Scotland.

Stronach's rendering of what kept the women of Scotland together and true to their role as keepers of their "hame" is beautifully stated in her own special way.

My mom was very proud of what she and other women did during the war; but she was proud in a way that was "matter of fact." All the women were in those circumstances together. It wasn't pride that she was a hero; that she was doing anything special or unusual. But, rather, a real sense of contribution and accomplishment. I believe she truly became aware of her strengths and abilities and of those around her as well. One of the things that awes me is how amazingly well these women got along with each other, despite living so closely together in cold, damp, drafty barracks under stressful conditions (having only two or three pieces of coal with which to try to keep themselves warm); regardless of how their differences were. Some of these women, like her friend Rennie, came from upper crust British background. Here she was with my mother, a country blacksmith's daughter—fast becoming best friends, actually, lifelong best friends. Rennie, also was a war bride; married my father's best friend, a wild fighter pilot, and ended up living within blocks of my parents in Toronto.

I gave Stronach the opportunity to express her own heartfelt sentiments on how her mother's role in WWII impacted her personally and its influence on her life. Here is Stronach's beautiful tribute to her mother, Betty O'Neil.

My mother was a wonderful story teller. Her tales of WWII were a delightful combination of heart, humor and mischief and so alive in the telling that we felt as if we were reliving the experience with her. Through the "war stories," I came to understand and honor the depth and breadth of her compassion, her courage, her feistiness, her wild abandon, her passion.

To say that my mother's participation in WWII affected me greatly is a huge understatement. Quite simply, I would not be here. It was while she, a young Highland Scot, was stationed in England that she met, courted and married my Canadian father. After the war, she, a war bride, bravely left her homeland and crossed the great ocean, with me, an end of the war baby in tow. As a young child in Canada, I was enthralled by her "adrenalin packed war adventures." During my prepubescence, her "love and relationship stories," especially those involving me, were captivating. As one, we partied and danced with joie de vivre, knowing that this moment might be the last. In adolescence, a sense of power and accomplishment satisfied my cool teenage pride. Vicariously, I donned leather and sped with her on a motorcycle; double clutched to perfection a huge lorry; raced wounded airmen to safety. As a young adult, I accompanied my parents on a "roots journey" to England and Scotland. The war came alive for me once more; however, this time it existed within an expanded paradigm of the relationship between violence and oppression, particularly of women. At that point in my life, I was securely and, I fear, somewhat smugly planted on the pedestal of my feminist platform. Initially, I began to view my mother in her current life through a narrow lens of judgment, and quite frankly, found her lacking. What actually evolved from that trip was a humbling awakening. The shell of "the acquiescing wife" was laid bare to reveal the core of a strong, autonomous woman who, as she so aptly demonstrated during WWII, was capable of doing anything with ingenuity, strength, dignity, grace, and a wicked sense of humor. I know my mother would put it this way: that she was only one of countless numbers of such capable, courageous women. (O'Neil: Gulfport, Florida, February 12, 2011)

Lynn Puzio—daughter of Sarah Cooper

Lynn Puzio was one of the Scottish immigrants I met through the Daughters of Scotia. Lynn initially thought she had little to contribute as she was born just before war was declared in 1939, but her mother had worked in munitions and as it turned out, Lynn had lots to say. I interviewed Lynn Puzio via telephone at her home in Pennsylvania on December 17, 2009. Lynn was born in '39 in Glasgow, Scotland, to Sarah Cooper who was nineteen at the time. Sarah's husband was called up to serve in the British Royal Navy as a Royal Marine, leaving her and their newborn baby to face the oncoming war.

Aye, I was born in '39 in Myerson Street in Possilpark, Glasgow. My dad was called up not too long after I was born. He was a marine in the British Royal Navy. So he was gone for a long time. It was hard. The war was on, but my mom always made everything happy. She always made everything light— made it so you didn't worry about things. A lot of the women, at that time, did that. I guess they were all feart, I think basically scared, trying not to impart that on their children. But what ah do remember was the air raids and having tae go tae the shelters. We used tae go in the back court, you know all the tenements had these big shelters. The sirens would come on and we'd all go doon tae the shelters. I must have been very young but I remember that as vividly as any memory that I have. I remember the sirens and getting all bundled up, going down the stairs in the shelter, sitting, hugging each other, and stuff. But again, my mother was a great personality lady. She used to keep everybody laughing. You had to be quiet though. You were supposed to be kind of quiet, not to make too much noise. But my mum did her best tae keep us from being too scared. She tried to make it not too much of a big deal, being in the shelter.

Having a young child kept Sarah Cooper from serving in the war effort but by 1943 every available woman was conscripted to serve in some capacity for their country. Sarah was fortunate in that her mother was available to care for her daughter Lynn while she worked in a local munitions factory in Glasgow. Lynn was unable to remember the name of the factory, but with some research, I was able to determine that her mother worked for Clydesdale Iron Works, a steel company that dealt mainly in structural steel and bridge building. But like many of the steel companies in Britain, they opened up munitions factories manufacturing the much needed ammunition, guns, Howitzer shells, and explosives.

My mum's work was in the munitions factory on Hawthorne Street, right doon the road from us. It was like an Iron Foundry. I can't remember the name of the place but I know all the women came out with their turbans, their hair all done up in their rollers and every night you'd see them come out of the foundry doors then be off tae have some fish and chips for dinner and maybe a movie. But I had a grandmother and a grandfather and two uncles who were like brothers to me. I kind of lived with them during the day while my mum was at work. She'd walk doon the road from the works and pick me up and take me home. My mother had a group of ladies, four or five of them that kept to themselves. They were a happy group. Everybody would come up to the house and have a coupla wee wines and they all would sit and talk. It wisnae a drastic time for us really. They were all young girls and they seemed to have lots of confidence. They were glad to be doing something. My mum was always a confident person and she was very, very smart. A very smart lady. She was the top of her class in school. She worked in some shop in Glasgow for a wee while then got pregnant with me. But she loved tae work even after the war she always worked. I think that helped give her confidence for she always had jobs where she was in charge of distribution or transporting things. I used to wonder about that—her being so confident 'cause my mum was a wee fat woman, she was very heavy. She didn't dress especially nice. She always had the same wee work frock, you know how they

*did in the auld days? But she always had a confidence about
her. She always managed to keep a good job going.*

In talking about her mom's confident and independent nature,
Lynn describes a very special person who had a love for life, a person
who gave her all for her country and her family. Lynn tells a very sad
ending to this life. It was if her mother knew she didn't have much
time and had to squeeze out the very best of every minute she had.

*When my mum was in school, besides being the top of
her class, she had a great voice too. They used to tell her she
should go and take singing lessons. Of course in those days, my
grandmother said: "Singing lessons? Get your arse oot there
and make some money." But she always sang. She loved to sing.
But she died awful young. She died at age fifty-six of breast
cancer. It was very, very sad. She went to the doctors two or
three times. They kept saying: "Oh, it's in yer mind." This was
in 1977, and they didn't know much about cancer then. Over
there, you didn't argue with the doctor, you just did what they
told you. Not like today where you can question everything.
She died fast, in nine months, she died. That was a tragedy
really. It was very hard for me. My father had died at age for-
ty-four. He was never right after the war. He could never settle
down. But I had my uncles and my grandparents' tae help me.
They were always there for me.*

Lynn continued to talk about how important the work that the
women did during the war. She not only has love and admiration for
the job her mother did but enormous respect for all the women who
gave so much.

*Ye know some of the women didnae think they could do
it. Yet they did it without any experience, without any training. They just stepped in there and did the job. They found
they could do the job that men were doing and it gave them
added confidence, a booster to take other jobs after the war was
over. That was true of a lot of women at the time. There were
women who had a lot of children. One of my neighbors had
nine children. She stayed at home wi her kids. But basically
folk with one or two children were out working, doing what-*

ever they could for the war effort and then even after the war was over.

There were good memories and memories that haunt Lynn to this day—memories that have made a lifetime impact on her.

> *There is a day I'll never forget: the day the war ended! Everybody came home early and put flags out. I'll never forget that. Everybody was out in the streets singing and dancing around. It was fantastic. It really was. I think I'll remember that 'til I die—that day! My mum came home early from work. Her pal came wi' her. We got her kids and then we all went out in the street dancing wi everybody. It was just a happy time.*
>
> *People talk about how Glasgow didn't get hit that bad wae bombs, but they didnae live in Glasgow at that time. Sometimes, we did get bombed or Clydebank got bombed, but there were always planes flying over, every night and ye never knew if they were going to hit ye. You know you don't even know what's happening to you at that age, but aw these years when I hear a plane going over, I tense up. My stomach tightens up. My husband and I lived in Long Island for forty years, and our house must have been in the flight path of the aircraft—taking off from the local airport. Every time a plane would go overhead, ma stomach would tighten up. So you don't even know it's happening to you. It just stays wi' ye all the time.*

I asked Lynn one last question: "What would you want the readers of this book to know about your experiences or your mom's experiences during the war? What would be the one thing you'd really like them to walk away with?"

> *I think it built character in both the child and the parent. I think it gave the parent a way to figure out that they could do this. They could live through this. They could manage to do it. And the child saw this and I think it gave people character and strength. They came out of it. It was a helluva war although a lot of people were killed, it was terrible, but it was a war worth fighting for! It gave you STRENGTH! Made you feel that you*

WOMEN WARRIORS OF WWII

could do anything! So as bad as it was, it may have helped some people, people that might never have attained anything in their life—found there wasn't anything they couldn't do. *I think I learned that from my mother, and hopefully, passed it onto my daughter. I encouraged my daughter Michele to be a doctor. I always thought: "Why marry a doctor, be a doctor. You can do whatever you want if you put your mind to it." And she did! My wee wain became a medical doctor. Her granny would be very proud!* (Puzio: Pennsylvania, USA, December 17, 2009)

Margaret Brown Reid—daughter of Margaret Gray Reid

Margaret, known as Peggy, is my sister and a major contributor to this book. She travelled with me to Scotland on many occasions to do research, interviewing some of the women, collecting data, taking pictures, and transcribing recordings of the interviewees. My sister's role has been invaluable, but just as importantly, she has some stories to tell about our mother. Having been born in 1935 in a Glasgow tenement, Peggy experienced the war years in Glasgow along with our older brother who was born in 1933. Our father was called up to serve when war was declared in 1939, leaving our mother as head of the household—caring for her two children, ages four and six. I was yet to come.

When dad left for the front, it was very hard on our mother, but she would never show that. During the war, the women of Scotland were stoic; displaying over and over again their fortitude in the face of danger, not only to themselves but to their families. She was no longer working. She was spending her time caring for us when we weren't in school and taking care of the household. But we had a very close family. My mother's sisters—Nancy, Belle, and Jean, and our granny Brown lived a few streets away.

My mother raised her family under the most stressful conditions; the blackouts, rationing of food, carrying gas masks, air raid shelters, the barrage balloons, and of course, the relentless fear of the bombings. I remember one of the many nights; the sirens rousing my brother and I. There was my mom standing

123

in the darkness, at the window, the blackout curtains shoved aside—we could see the searchlights in the sky. With the bombs raining down on us, my mom gathered my brother and me up and we fled to our air raid shelter.

Happily for me, my father was allowed a visit home after the battle of Dunkirk. Being part of the British Expeditiary Force filled my father with pride, but also sadness as he had lost many of his mates in battle. His making it home was a blessing to us all. It was a short visit, but a significant one—nine months later I was born.

My mother became pregnant during one of my father's rare visits home during the war and my sister was born during our evacuation to Fauldhouse in 1941. Returning to Glasgow we, soon after, moved to Possilpark to another tenement apartment, but one that was a wee bit bigger. Now our mother had a new born to care for as well as a six-and-eight-year-old. Fortunately, my brother and I were at school all day, which was a big help to her, especially while the baby was still so young.

Although the focus of this book is the role women played during WWII, another relevant feature emphasized repeatedly through these women's voices is the impact on the children that endured the appalling stressors bestowed on them. Many children, boys and girls, lost their childhood—having to grow up way too soon—taking on the role of a parent. My brother Tom was one of those children. He, very quickly, became "the man of the house" taking on the very important role of caring and protecting his two wee sisters. By age ten, he had two other jobs—delivering milk to the tenements and delivering newspapers to local customers. He was a tough wee Glaswegian. He had to be!

So much was expected of us at such young age that it made us extremely responsible. Don't complain, "get on wae it" was the Glasgow motto. As children, we shared a common lot with our peers, we gave up a part of our childhood to help our mother's involvement in the war effort. As school age children, we knitted, went into the fields to harvest the strawberries and other fruits and vegetables. I remember a German POW helping me fill the punnets as it was a backbreaking job. We watched over our siblings, queued for our rations, and helped at home with the cooking and cleaning. We became fiercely governed by a no-nonsense conscience: being dutiful, dependable, diligent, loyal, and efficient.

By early 1942, the pressure was on every British woman, married or single, to register with the Ministry of Labor. My aunt Belle had joined the ARP and my aunt Jean was working as a porter at Glasgow Central Train Station. But my mother and aunt Nancy were not quite ready to leave their household as I was only six months old, and my aunt Nancy was pregnant and due any minute. By 1943, life was dire in Britain—anyone and everyone was needed. I was almost two years old when my mother decided she had to do something. Luckily, nursery schools were available to mothers with young children. Thus, it became Tom and Peggy's job to take me to the nursery school every day. From my understanding, it was a heart wrenching chore as I cried the whole way there—you see, "I wisnae daft, I knew where I was going even at two years of age."

One of the more critical and important areas that needed workers was in transportation—the Trams. My mother signed up to be a driver but she kept failing the driver's test, so she trained instead to be a conductress, or as was called in those days, a "Clippie." My aunt Nancy joined my mom in this endeavor and became a Tram driver. When my mom migrated to America, she tried her best to learn how to drive an American car on the "wrong" side of the road. She lived to be seventy-three and never did learn how to drive. But that never stopped her from getting to where she had to go. She always worked and would use all kinds of public transportation to get to her job— including NYC subways, buses, and trains.

My mother was a "Clippie." She wore a uniform, carried a large leather bag over her shoulder which held change and tickets and which was very heavy, and she was on her feet all day. She worked as a conductress on the trams. There were long shifts, she was up and down the stairs multiple times a day, had to call out the stops, and deal with tired, fearful people. At the same time, she ran her home with three children while her husband was off to war. She faced all of this with the stoicism that is uniquely Scottish. Sometimes, my mother brought her full, heavy shoulder bag home with her, particularly if she had another shift as was often the case. The temptation was always there "tae us wee yins" to help ourselves to a penny or two, BUT as my mother explained to my brother and I; at the end of each shift, she had to resolve the cash and the tickets sold. If they did not and a shortage ensued, she had to pay the difference out of her pay. Temptation soon faded quickly.

One evening, following a grueling day, our mother shared one of her demanding events. The Americans had come to Scotland, and of course, were riding the trams. One of a party of them asked my mother if she would like some popcorn. Thinking of us, she responded, "Yes!" She had it with her and we all looked at these tiny kernels. Being totally ignorant as to what to do with them, we did as most Scottish folk would do; we threw them in the fire. What a calamity! Tiny balls while making a mild explosive sound, started flying out of the fire all over us. We had a good laugh when all was said and done. To this day, the popping and smell of popcorn reminds me of that day.

Conductresses and drivers of the Trams were essential jobs usually carried out by men. A woman taking on this job was most unusual and the fact that they did it and did it well also gives credence to fact that they received equal pay as the men—an incredible occurrence. Women brought their personality and fortitude to the job, and in the words of Ian Nimmo in Scotland at War: "Glamour came to the trams in Glasgow."

As I have done with all the women I interviewed, I asked my sister Peggy: "How do you feel about our mother's role in the war and how has that impacted you and your life?"

Looking back as an adult, I am filled with pride and awe when I think of my mother and the war years. Raising a family under normal circumstances was a job in itself, however, raising a family, giving birth, moving, and working a job regularly held by a man, all under war conditions, was by any standards, a Herculean task. Remember this was done while my father was away and only home on sporadic leaves. Mom did it all!

How has this impacted me? As a child of the second world war, I was imbued with a sense of urgency that pervaded every aspect of my life from eating as if it was my last meal to a neurotic sense of time. How so, well, I was always in a hurry, always on time, and every task started was well organized and completed on schedule. This served me well later in life! As a career woman, I was good at my job. Always willing and an ardent role model for bringing out the best in others—not only in their achievements but their productivity as well. As a responsible being, I brought people together as a team that got the job done; A matter of "getting on wae it." My work ethic was prodigious and that bred success.

My mother made a magnificent contribution to womanhood. Multiply her efforts by thousands, and you have a legacy that goes on for generations. She confronted the barriers facing her resolutely with courage, endurance, and perseverance. I wish I had known her better, but she left a legacy that withstands the minutest scrutiny. She was a woman for all ages. We may ask, "What did she do for the war effort?" My answer is simple. She gave herself which was formidable! (Reid: Ayr, Scotland, June 26, 2012)

Margaret G. Reid in "Clippie" uniform

Mary Scharosch: Daughter of Elizabeth Connelly and niece of Anne Nimmo

Having met Mary Scharosch through my sister Peggy, we were able to set up a telephone interview in February, 2010. Mary was born in June of 1940 in Glasgow, Scotland, to Elizabeth "Betty" Connelly. It was Betty's second child, her first, a son, was born in 1937. Betty's husband was in the British Merchant Marines, a job that became not only consequential, but extremely dangerous during WWII. As the war progressed, she saw less and less of her husband and had to take on the role as head of the household, raising two young children in the middle of a major battleground—Glasgow and Clydebank.

I was born June 1940. My mother told me she went into labor the morning of June 20, and that her neighbor and best friend, Jean MacMillan, was with her during her labor. Jean lived in the landing below, thank goodness, as the air raids were going every day. In the war time, you had to notify the midwife—we had no phones—and she would come by to check you out. No doctor was available because the hospitals were for the wounded, not for delivering babies. A midwife examined my mum during the day and said it would be hours before delivery. The Germans attacked that evening dropping bombs on Glasgow. Jean delivered me during the air raid. Can you imagine a young woman having to deliver during an air raid? I am sure it happened to many young women during the war, but the strength it must have taken to avoid total panic for a new mother and those who were caring for the women in labor. The midwife came the next day to check on us and make up the birth certificate for the doctor to sign making my birth official. Mrs. MacMillan was a lifelong friend of my mother's staying close to our family throughout the years no matter how far away we were. They always wrote and sent cards and presents back and forth during that time. She would often send me letters signed, "Your wee Scots, Mum."

My mother said that she basically had to do everything during the war. She took care of us, of course, during the war, but there were few men around. We had one man on the landing, they wouldn't allow him to go to war because he was a mechanic and he worked for the transportation department. He kept all the trams and everything running. So they kept him at home! He was the only man in their close, so he did all the odd jobs. He was a wonderful help. My mother said that they were really difficult years and that the air raids were awful. They were bombed so many times because where they lived was near the Clyde and the bombers would just fly over our streets. We lived off of London Road by Strathy's Park in a tenement on Williamson Street and our view was of that park. I can still remember looking out the window and seeing the park.

My mother said that the air raids were so frequent; she became exhausted waking up my older brother and me and taking us to the shelters almost every night. She decided if her time was up, she was going in her own house so she did not go to the shelters ever again. I think one reason was her step-mother was in a shelter when a bomb hit her building. Her shelter was between two large rows of tenements and the shelter was buried by the bombings. Her stepmom had to be dug out. She survived, but the memory of this made a big impact on my mother. Williamson Street was very close to the Clyde so many bombs were dropped in that area and our windows were blown out frequently.

The air raids were very frightening to my mother and she wanted to protect us as much as she could. My mother was very close with the Irish side of our family—my mother's stepmother and brothers—who were living in Larne, Ireland, during the war. They were very good to my mother and my brother and I. We used to go there, especially with the bombing being so bad, as often as we could. My dad, being a merchant seaman was often away for long periods. When my dad would leave, my mom said, he wasn't down the street before she would be packing her suitcase. She would pack us all up, and then we would take the train, then the boat over to Larne. She went at night when the boats had to run without lights so they wouldn't be bombed. Now she is taking care of two kids, it's in the dark, with a chance of being bombed or hitting a mine. But she took the chance. And she went a lot. That's where my mom would take us when she could get away. She didn't do it just because of the bombing; it was the whole situation because of the shortage of food in Glasgow. My mother's family lived near the farms outside of Larne. There was milk for us, and eggs, all the things she couldn't get at home. That's where my mother went. It was sort of a refuge for her.

Mary talks about another important person in her life, her aunt Anne, her mother's only sister, and only living sibling. Betty and Anne lost their mother, Mary's grandmother, when she was twenty-six years old. She died when she was pregnant with her seventh child in seven years. Of the seven children, the girls were the only two that survived, the five boys died in infancy. Thus bringing the two sisters very close, very connected to each other.

My Aunt Anne was a big influence in my life. She had such spirit and I adored her. Aunt Anne and my mother were very close even though my mom was older by three and half years. After their mother died, their father remarried. Aunt Anne had problems with her stepmother so she left home at age fifteen. She first lived in a pension run by a church, and then got a job in a fruit shop at the end of our street. I loved having my auntie in the shop so close to our house, and she would come up for her tea. I remember my Aunt Anne making toffee apples for the children on our street. Mother said my aunt would collect sugar from the neighbors who would save a little each week from their rations, and when there was enough, and she had apples, she would make them in the shop and hand them out to the lucky children.

When she was a called up at age seventeen and half, she chose the Women's Auxiliary Air Force (WAAF). At first, they had her doing bookkeeping which she absolutely couldn't do because she just sat in a room by herself just counting numbers. So they sent her for further training; packing parachutes for a while and then learning how to refuel airplanes. She was eventually sent to Dover, England, which had special landing strips for airmen who were flying back home and ran out of fuel or who were really close but couldn't make it back to their squadron. *They would then land on this air strip. Aunt Anne would get a call from her commander, pedal out on her bicycle from some Quonset hut where she had to stay, and she would refuel the airplanes. She did this in all kinds of weather and spent many nights waiting for a call to help the airmen. So she really enjoyed chatting with the pilots while refueling their planes whenever she got that call.*

My Auntie Anne was a fun loving person. She and a bunch of girls from the air base—you know they were all young—really wanted to go to this dance in the town. They would not have been allowed to go, so she got someone to cover the fueling in case there was an emergency. But Auntie Anne didn't think there would be a problem for it wasn't a very good night for flying as the weather was bad. She said they snuck out of their Quonset hut, went over the fence, and into town. They danced 'til the wee hours of the morning having a great time. They were walking back when a fire truck came by and picked them up and took them to their base and dropped them off. Of course, all the girls were worried that they would be in trouble with the sergeant that was in charge of them. They wondered if the woman really realized they were gone and just let them go and didn't say anything; or if they were in deep trouble and going to be kicked out of the service. Then the girls thought, "Why would they kick us out? They really need us!"

Aunt Anne experienced a lot in the war. She was injured about the last year of the war. She slipped on some ice and fell while on duty in England and it damaged her kidneys. She had to have a kidney removed and was hospitalized there with young airmen for almost a year. She always laughed about her recovery program. She was always a thin woman anyway, but she got very, very thin. Her doctor put her on a very interesting diet. They wanted her to eat well, so she was fed well, but she had to have a pint of stout with her lunch and her dinner. And she hated it! So she would give it to the young airmen in the hospital who were very happy to take it off her hands. And then they told her to start smoking cigarettes every day to calm her nerves. She didn't like that either, so she gave her cigarettes to the airmen too making her quite popular. After a year of hospitalization, she came home and the war ended a few months later. It is amazing what they considered medically sound in those years! My Aunt Anne never ever became a smoker. She and my mom were two very strong women. Over the years, both had breast cancer and both were survivors. My mother lived until she was ninety-three and my aunt lived until she was eighty-seven. And that was just with one kidney!

The two sisters were inseparable eventually emigrating to America after the war. They had a great aunt who had come to America years before WWII and in one of her visits home she convinced Anne to move there and she would sponsor her. It didn't take much convincing—Anne was off to America! Once she was established in her new country, Anne wrote her sister Betty, "You need to come and bring the kids." Mary tells a funny, but ironic, anecdote of her mother's preparation for emigrating to America.

My mother's mind was made up. She wanted so much to join my aunt in this new adventure. These sisters had a lot of courage and were not afraid to face the unknown. My dad was still at sea, but my mother was determined to move to America, so when he came home she told him. He said: "No, he had already been there as he shipped in and out of San Francisco and different New York ports. I am not going to do that." She said, "Well I am going to go with or without you." I thought that was pretty gutsy for my mother to say. And what my dad didn't know was that my mother had already applied for emigration. Once she received notification that her application was confirmed, she had to apply ahead of time for a boat reservation. She went ahead and put her name in for a date. When she received confirmation of the sailing date, she told my dad, "I am going and this is the date." She put his name in too. So he came. Grumbled all the way! For many years, he grumbled. He didn't like it here. He said to her, "For God's sake, you could nae even pick a place near an ocean?" Here he was up in Sacramento and he could have joined the Merchant Marines and sailed out of San Francisco. But he never did that! I don't know why he didn't but he always talked about it because he didn't like being away from the sea. My mother wanted to be near her sister. They wanted to stay together, the sisters. They really did! So it was a wee bit sad for my dad. But he did have a choice; he could have continued to be a Merchant Marine— in a different country, the USA.

Life in American suited the sisters well. It was a new adventure, one filled with excitement and wonder. Both took on new jobs, working hard to have a glorious life with many new friends.

My mother was looking for something better. When she came here, she'd not worked when we were in school in Scotland, so she thought she might as well do something. She and my father were starting over and my mom wanted her own home, so she went to work as a waitress and she'd never done anything like that. But she told them, "I know I can do it." Then she wanted a better job so she got a job as a postmistress. She'd never done anything like that either. She just continued to work her way up—next to the department of motor vehicles for the state where she knew she could get a pension and health benefits. My mum was very strong. She knew what she wanted and went and got it! My aunt was the same but she always had a job and always found a way to make money. Like the time she was on this base and she had a sewing machine. So she said, "I looked around and saw all these young airmen, and I thought, there's no way any of them could put their stripes on their uniforms." So she started a little business sewing on their stripes. It was really good for her as she made money while she was there, kept her busy, and she had company as these guys would come in and chat with her while she sewed their stripes on. She always found a way to work and make money. She was quite an entrepreneur!

I asked Mary what she thought about her mother's role in WWII and how that impacted her, her life, and her children. Her answer speaks volumes, not only for her and her family, but for all the Scottish women who gave so much for their family and country.

My mother's role in WWII was typical for a young married woman with two very young children. Her attitude impacted my life in many ways. Her ability to cope with any situation and resolve the issue in a creative way, I am sure, was shaped by the war. Surviving WWII gave her confidence in her ability to survive any situation and as she said, "Just get on wae it." Without fear of the unknown gives you the ability to move ahead to forge new paths which she did by journeying to America with not much more than hope for a better life for her family.

After 9/11, my mother and I were going to fly to Missouri to visit my daughter. I asked my mother, how could she fly when someone on the plane might be a terrorist or have a bomb? My mother said: "No one is going to scare me out of visiting my granddaughter; after all I survived the blitz." After the blitz, what is one bomb threat? She was never hesitant about flying and nothing much scared her because she felt she had already faced more danger than most people would ever encounter. She said she would never give "those people" the satisfaction of scaring her into changing her life and what she wanted to do.

My Aunt's experience as a member of WAAF must have contributed to her ability to do almost anything, any place, with anyone and with great humor. She was a great influence in my life with her "can do" approach to life. I believe confidence comes with positive accomplishments at a young age. If at seventeen you can ride alone through a storm on a bike, in the dark, on a remote lane in England to gas up a lone fighter plane, you can do anything life presents.

I see in my children and grandchildren the confidence to analyze a situation, and "Just get on wae it." They all have the ability to get along with anyone and never appear to be daunted by issues. Both of my children have graduate degrees and the grandchildren are now graduating from the university and applying for graduate degrees. Each one has had challenges which they have met with humor and the ability to go forward with determination. I think it is in their genes, and I am thankful for my mother and Aunt Anne who were women that set the pattern for success in life by accepting any chal-

lenge with dignity, pride, and a creative approach to living. I believe that British women were the backbone of their country in WWII. They were overlooked and certainly did not receive a medal for their courage. No matter what, they were determined to survive—and they did! (Scharosch: Sacramento, California, February 3, 2010)

These stories have depicted the voices of the daughters of the women who served during WWII, extraordinary ones at that! It was as if they were living the times all over again—it was so real. Incredibly, the women were young again, conveying the same responses, the same sensitivity, and the same impact that had influenced their entire lives. These are exemplary women, enduring an unimaginable existence in their formative years—a period that not only made an imprint on them but their children and grandchildren. "Just get on wae it" has been passed on to many generations of Scots.

CHAPTER 9
I REALIZED THERE WASN'T ANYTHING I COULDN'T DO

VE Day, May, 8, 1945—the war is over! In Britain, everyone was dancing in the streets. Husbands, brothers, uncles, nephews, and some sisters and mothers too, would soon be home although many would not be demobbed until 1946. The women of the Timber Corps and Land Army continued to produce the wood and food which was still badly needed well into 1946, in fact, food rationing was still going on in Britain until the '50's. It was going to take a number of years before Britain could get back on its feet. As the men returned home from combat, they were given back the jobs promised to them and the women who had taken over these jobs were forced to give them up. This was a difficult predicament for numerous women. Most of them were willing to move on and get back to their former life, but there were also large numbers of women who wanted to work—needed to work—as life in post war Britain was bleak, encouraging many to immigrate—looking for a better life.

Thousands of young British women met and married military men from the United States, Canada, Australia, and New Zealand, who had been stationed in Britain during the war. Some of the marriages or expectations of marriage did not turn out well, but a great deal of them—as was told by the interviewees—went on to live long and happy lives with their beloved husbands. There were also English and Scottish families—such as mine—who had a relative in the United States or Canada who was willing to sponsor them. Thus, allowing the family to immigrate there and begin a new life. This was very much a trend after the war—the great migration! But the majority of the Scots remained in their homeland, having children, raising their families, with husbands and wives working to make a better life a priority.

Population in Britain, pre and post WWII was approximately forty-seven million people with a little over half being women. In Scotland, the population in 1939 was 5,006,700 and by 1951, it rose to 5,096,000 even with many migrating to other countries. Married couples being separated for many years due to the war brought on a significant influx of children into the world; thus, the beginning of the "Baby Boomer Generation." Life was changing in Scotland. Winning the hard fought war brought a great amount of relief to all, but the manner in which it occurred—sacrifices made, courage it took, and dedication to their country—resulted in women feeling more confident about themselves and their future. Education not only became increasingly important to them with many women returning to college, but education also became paramount for their children. Giving up their jobs at war's end was not acceptable—working and having a job was first and foremost to many of the Scottish women, which also contributed to the changing life in Scotland. It was a new dawn, a new way of looking at things. These women were looking through a new lense—one that said: "There isn't anything you can't do!"

What you have experienced in reading these women's stories is a snapshot of history—a desperate time—a moment that required extreme measures. For the ruler of Nazi Germany, Adolf Hitler, a psychotic narcissist was driven to be "king" of the world. Hitler, unhesitatingly rolling over Europe one country at a time, was fixated on conquering Britain. After all, Great Britain and its Commonwealth nations had the reputation of being a world power with a formidable army and navy. Hitler was determined to bringing them down by relentless bombings and intimidating tactics toward the British people. But lo and behold, something unperceived happened. When the Brits' backs were to the wall, every available man was removed from every necessary job at home to go to the war front. These jobs had to be filled and they were—by their women!

This was an astounding event—women were actually going to do a man's job. Women were called upon in the Great War to do minimal tasks—tasks that were generally accepted as women's jobs, i.e. cooks, waitresses, instructors, *telephonists*, but in WWII, that ceiling was broken. An inconceivable door had been thrust open. It was unimaginable what these young women—teenagers to early twenties mostly—ended up doing as if it were "nothing"—no big deal! We saw this in the Scottish women's stories how they "just got on wae it"—a formidable way of looking at life. They took on a way of life that was totally new to them, actually performing chores, missions, responsibilities that they never in their wildest dreams thought they would be called upon to do. Not only did they do these jobs but they did them with minimum training, and in some cases, no training. But the kicker is these women were exceptional, profound, multitalented, remarkable, discerning, skilled, and wise.

During the war years, the Women's Land Army produced twice the amount of food that was available before the war; WTC were unrelenting with the wood they provided for telegraph poles, fire arms, railway sleepers and ties, pit props for coal mines, munitions factories, and coffins; Women in the ATS drove eighteen-wheeler lorries delivering food and supplies, ambulances, and driving generals to top secret locations, some of them were even called upon as part of the Expeditiary Force in France; WRNS began as drivers and clerks but as the war progressed, they helped maintain the Royal Navy ships and some were involved in the most secret planning for D-Day; WAAFs were working in the Royal Observer Corps, and some in special operations as saboteurs, couriers, and radio operators; nurses worked in military field hospitals—at times near the front lines of battle; Cyphering jobs were mostly done by women—they had a unique ability to intercept German coded messages and decipher them; hundreds of thousands of women worked in the dangerous munitions factories, inhaling hazardous chemicals, and at times, losing a limb or their life due to an explosion; For the first time, women were actually working in the shipyards—building ships, working as electricians, welders, forgers, soldering damaged engines, and on and on; our women took on the trams as drivers and "Clippies"; they were Air Raid Wardens protecting families, elderly folk, and the disabled—keeping the neighborhoods safe; and then we have the soul of the country—the women who were at home caring for their children, keeping them safe, healthy, and strong, for they were the future of their country. All these women took over every conceivable job that was required to keep the country going, yet they never received the recognition they deserved. This was a daunting task that the women of Britain took on, but took it on they did and with great valor and success!

More than half of the Earth's population is made up of females—infants, girls, young women, and elderly women—yet they do not get the recognition, acceptance, support, admiration that the males get—the other half of our planet. This has been going on for thousands of years. What is it going to take for women to get the recognition they deserve?

The world has not changed much since those war years of 1939–1945. Although the number of British women continuing to work increased after the war as it was necessary to survive, but also they had much more confidence in their ability to hold a job and do it well. There was also a substantial increase in the number of young women going onto university—again, that feeling that there wasn't anything they couldn't do, drove them to higher dreams. Unfortunately, seventy years later since the end of WWII, women throughout the world still struggle just to get an education. Even in "advanced" countries such as United Kingdom of Britain, United States of America, Canada, Australia and the countries in the European Union, women are not treated fairly in the workforce compared to men—being paid less for the same job as a man, with less women in managerial or professional jobs, very few women as head of companies, and even fewer women as leaders of nations.

Over fifty million people died in World War II, some of them British, but Scottish, English, and Welsh women would not allow their country to die—they stood their ground proving under the direst of circumstances that women are capable of doing whatever is necessary to get the job done. This is the message of this book—told by the Women Warriors of World War II, and being passed on to the young women of today—that there isn't anything you can't do. Your time has come—to take on a more proactive role for women's rights, recognition, and acceptance as an equal in today's world.

GLOSSARY

Ack Ack Unit: Military abbreviation for antiaircraft artillery unit.

ARP: Air Raid Precautions

ARW: Air Raid Wardens

ATS: Auxiliary Territorial Service

Barrage Balloons: A bag of lighter-than-air gas attached to a steel cable anchored to the ground used ingenuously during WWII. Barrage Balloons were fixed throughout Glasgow and Clydebank area, London and surrounding areas, forcing enemy aircraft to fly at higher altitudes, thereby decreasing surprise and bombing accuracy. The cables anchoring the balloons provided a definite hazard to any low flying planes. By August of 1940, 2,368 Barrage Balloons were used throughout Britain where it was necessary to protect civilians and factory areas.

Bletchley Park: Britain's main decryption station where they broke the codes (the secret communications of the Germans) which made a major impact on Germany's attempt to conquer the world.

Blitzkrieg: German word depicting the massive bombardment of major cities in Britain—cities such as London, Manchester, Glasgow, Clydebank where there were masses of people, ship building, and factories.

Bow and Arrow Antiaircraft Unit: Antiaircraft units had their own badge to distinguish them from each other—Bow and Arrow was one of them

Byre: A cow barn

Ciphering: Decoding messages

Demobbed: Demobilization, to discharge a person from the armed services

Doodle Bugs: Nickname for German unmanned flying bomb

DOS: Daughters of Scotia, a woman's organization formed in the United States by Scottish women who had immigrated to America.

Drifters: Type of fishing boat used in Oban, Scotland

Ferranti's: A chief supplier of electronics, fuses, valves, and a major player in the development of radar in Britain in WWII. In 1943, they opened a factory at Crewe Toll in Edinburgh manufacturing Gyro Gunsights for the Spitfire aircraft.

Glaswegian: A native of Glasgow, Scotland

Howitzer Shells: Shell of bullet used in Howitzer artillery gun. A special type of artillery piece used to attack at long range and with a high angle so it could land over a fortification.

Kriegsmarine: The German Navy—the equivalent of the British Royal Navy, or U.S. Navy

NAAFI: Navy, Army, Air Force Institutes—an organization created by the British government in 1921 to run recreational establishments needed by the British Armed Forces. During WWII, NAAFI ran over seven thousand canteens with over ninety-six thousand personnel (mostly women), providing food, goods, and drinks; along with comfort, social interaction, and a sense of home.

Operation Pied Piper: Name given to British government's evacuation plan for the children of Britain during WWII.

Phony War: Term given to the period of time in WWII, September 1939 to April 1940, where supposedly "nothing" was happening, at least not to the expectations of the British government.

RAF: Royal Air Force

Reserved Occupations: Key jobs which exempted certain skilled workers from conscription. These jobs covered five million men working in the railway, or as dockworkers, miners, farmers, agricultural workers, schoolteachers, and doctors. The British government did not want to make the same mistake they made in the Great War (WWI), conscripting all the men leaving major deficits in war production. But it proved to be a poor solution as all men were needed in WWII, requiring the women of Britain to take over the jobs.

Royal Observer Corps: Civilians, many of whom were women and even young boys, acted as the "eyes and ears" of the RAF. Often stationed on top of hills, their job was to be on the lookout for any aircraft flying over Britain most especially the German Lufwaffe.

Snedding: A term used by Scottish Highlanders felling trees. Snedding was stripping the buds and branches off a felled tree before hauling it away to the saw mill.

Tilley lamps: Storm lamps produced by the Tilley family in England beginning in 1920. Providing light and heat, Tilley lanterns were used extensively in the Highlands of Scotland during WWII and are still used to this day throughout the world.

V2 Rockets: German unmanned flying bomb. When flying overhead, V2 rockets made a loud double clap—a sound that brought instant fear to many.

WAAC: Women's Auxiliary Army Corps

WAAF: Women's Auxiliary Air Force

WRNS: Women's Royal Naval Service

REFERENCES

Black, N. (2007). *Courage: A Teenagers View of War.* Oban, Scotland: Nancy Black.

Chokshi, N. (2014, September 14). *Analysis of working women in United States.* Retrieved from

www.washingtonpost.com/blogs/govbeat.

Damer, S. (1989). *Glasgow for a Song.* England: Lawrence & Wishart Ltd.

Douglas, D. (1996). *At the Helm, the Life and Times of Dr. Robert D. McIntyre.* Scotland: NPFI Publications.

Dudgeon, P. (2009). *Our Glasgow.* London, England: Headline Review.

Eleven Hundred Killed in Clyde Raids. (1941, April 2). Glasgow Herald.

Gannon, P. (2006). *Colossus Bletchley Park's Greatest Secret.* Great Britain: Atlantic Books Ltd.

Goldsmith, M. (1942). *Women at War.* England: Lindsay Drummond Ltd.

Harris, C. (2000). *Women at War 1939-1945.* Thrupp, England: Sutton Press.

Harris, C. (2011, February 17). *Women Under Fire in WW2.* Retrieved from www.bbc.co.uk/history.

Hutton, G. (1994). *Old Maryhill.* United Kingdom: Stenlake Publishing.

McKay, S. (2010). *The Secret Life of Bletchley Park.* London, England: Aurum Press.

McKay, S. (2013). *The Secret Listeners*. London, England: Aurum Press.

Nemmo, I. (1989). *Scotland at War*. Edinburgh, Scotland: Archives Publication in Association with The Scotsman Publications.

Priestley, J.B. (1943). *British Women Go to War*. London, England: Collins Publishers.

Scott, P. (1944). *They Made Invasion Possible*. London, England: Hutchinson & Co Press.

Taylor, W.L. (2010). *A hive of activity*. Edinburgh, Scotland: Forestry Commission, pp 18-25.

Walding, R. (2010, October, 27). *Indicator Loops*. Retrieved from http://indicatorloops.com

Whittell, G. (2007). *Spitfire Women of WW2*. London, England: Harper Press.

ABOUT THE AUTHOR

Jeanette B. Reid, a recently retired Psychotherapist, is a first time author. Having been born in Scotland during World War II, she brings authenticity and passion to her book about the Scottish women who served their country. She and her immediate family immigrated to America in 1947, with some of her mother's siblings and families following a few years later. Dr. Reid currently lives in Florida, but has never forgotten the land of her birth, making many visits over the years.

CPSIA information can be obtained at www.ICGtesting.com
Printed in the USA
LVOW10s1002190416

484216LV00004B/13/P